Late-Night River Lights

A Collection of Stories by

Meleina Backhaus
Shannon Bates
Digby Beaumont
Chris Bell
Dan Coxon
William de Rham
Lauren Farnsworth
Tom Gant
Paolo Gardinali
Lawrence M. John
Jreamwriter
Bernadette Klubb
Matthew Louis
James Meredith
Anne Leigh Parrish
Jessica Phippen
Samantha Priestley
T. Rigney
Teri Davis Rouvelas
Alice Shin
Stacy Taylor
Nisha Woolfstein
Sarah Young

Edited by
Kelly Smith

EditRed

First published in Denmark in September 2007 by EditRed

Copyright © 2007 by EditRed

ISBN 978-0-6151-8062-5

EditRed
Dybbølsgade 14, st. th
1721 Copenhagen V

www.EditRed.com

For all the new lights...

Contents

Foreword
By Kelly Smith 6

A Slice of Nana's Sweet Potato Pie
By Jreamwriter 8

'Kind of Blue': A five-part seduction fantasy
By Chris Bell 12

Once Upon a Time the Medway Literati
By Lawrence John 20

The Apple
By Alice Shin 24

City Limits
By Meleina Backhaus 32

So Very Necessary
By Stacy Taylor 36

Blue Flowers
By T. Rigney 42

Baptisms
By Teri Davis Rouvelas 50

My Night at Rosie's
By William de Rham 58

Day Seven
By Dan Coxon 70

Barney Jones
By Samantha Priestley 78

Burden
By Shannon Bates 88

The Baby in the Cupboard
   By Paolo A. Gardinali   94

From Castlebar to Dundalk
   By Bernadette Klubb   102

Fred Fletcher
   By Matthew Louis   108

For The Taking
   By Anne Leigh Parrish   124

Garden Story
   By Nisha Woolfstein   140

Learning to Float
   By James Meredith   146

Two Men in a Car
   By Digby Beaumont   158

Wonderland
   By Sarah Young   164

The Silver Meseca
   By Tom Gant   172

What the Birds Say
   By Lauren Farnsworth   191

The Dictionary of Loneliness
   By Jessica Phippen   195

Contributors   205

Foreword
by Kelly Smith

We walk hand in hand through Bridge Street, the night air fresh, the city bustling. I glance quickly at *The Bookshop*, now closed down, shelves gaping empty where dusty books were once piled high. I remember the feel of them, texts that other hands have held, pages smooth and worn with the touch of other fingers, spines crumbling, covers falling away in your palm like butterfly scales. At home, another book awaits its own moment in time, now aglow from a computer screen on my office desk. Collected stories by collected authors are told across continents. Emails from Copenhagen and London await me, tales are told between cities.

Dodging cyclists, their bells ringing out a warning call, we cross the road and into the warmth of *The Pickerel Inn*. The only place to sit in this pub is at the window, to people-watch over a pint. Our drinks sit before us, a red wine and a Guinness, the glow of a single candle flickers on the worn wooden bench and lights up our faces, his features. We are in our own world. Outside, people hurry past. We give each person a story in our minds, who they are and where they are going. We giggle conspiratorially. Autumn is giving way to winter, early Christmas shoppers hurry home with new purchases. Two students, faces buried deep in their scarves, glance in our direction as they enter Magdalene College through the old stone entrance, its archway darkened. Michaelmas term is half way over; unlit Christmas lamps are strung high across the streets waiting to be brought to life.

Beyond the iron railings and the quayside gardens lies the bridge and, beyond that, the river. Late-night river lights are reflected in the calm waters. The punts are mere shadows, lined up in rows, wooden sides gently knocking together in the darkness. Our faces are mirrored in the window. We catch each other's eye, reflected in the glass, and we smile.

There is no place like this. People walking past watch us as we watch them. However short our story, right now it begins and ends like this. In a pub, on a street, in a city that we love; new lights emerging.

Kelly Smith
Cambridge, November 2007

A Slice of Nana's Sweet Potato Pie
By Jreamwriter

To get your man, give him a pretty smile; wear a pretty dress; give him plenty of your attention; laugh at all his jokes; spray on some Chantilly Lace; wear a purple orchid in your hair; (but what if his favorite color is red?) Listen to me child, this is a recipe, and all the ingredients are exact. A hard head makes a soft behind; don't end up like your momma, manning the fields; bailing the hay; milking the cows; mowing the grass; taking out the trash; and changing the oil on the old blue pickup, after slaughtering hogs in the morn to make sage-seasoned sausage to sell at the market.

(Nana, I don't reckon meeting my Daddy, so I guess Momma didn't get a man.) Your Momma got a man, but she did not keep her man; she did not listen to Nana. To keep you a man, always listen to your Nana; tell that man that you love him, and give him a slice of Nana's special sweet potato pie. (But Nana, I do not have a sweet potato pie.) Hush now! Make haste; there is much to do; he will be here at six.

You are a woman now, and will have to use your womanhood to make that man see that you are a rare find. Do you have that little black dress Nana made for you last year, the one you wore to your graduation? His eyes will fall plum out of his head when Nana takes it in at the sides and raises the hem. (But Nana, won't he then see my legs?) Easter Beagle, you have Nana's legs; of course, he will want to see them. Go into the back room, and ask Trixy for her thigh-high stockings, she won't need them, she doesn't have any prospects for a husband. Trixy is like your momma, she didn't listen to Nana either. Just like your momma, Trixy ended up manning the fields; bailing the hay; milking the cows; mowing the grass; taking out the trash; and changing the oil on the old blue pickup, after slaughtering hogs in the morn to make sage-seasoned sausage to sell at the market. Mind your Nana child, and you surely won't suffer like the ones before you.

Your hair is done up nice. Put the orchid on the right side of your head, just above your ear, that way your bangs will drape across your brow. That man will reach to move the misplaced strands of hair from your face in order to take a gander at those emerald green eyes; but do not let him get too close to your pretty face, he still has tracks on his teeth; they might cut your pretty lips when he tries to kiss you. (Do you really think my lips are pretty, Nana?) Child, do not ask silly questions, of course you do, you have Nana's lips.

You sure look pretty in that garment, Easter Beagle. Turn around and sashay in that dress. When a man sees a woman walk with a sway to her hips, he goes into a trance, like a snake being charmed by a snake charmer. (Nana, now that the dress is taken in a bit, I do see that I have hips.) Of course you do, Easter Beagle, you have Nana's hourglass shape from once upon a time.

Now, let me see that beam child; you have Nana's smile, so less is more. Remember that rule when you laugh at his jokes, don't show so much teeth, else, you'll scared the poor man away. Lets hopes that young man has a good sense of humor, Nana can't stand a boring gent.

That perfume sure smells good on you Easter Beagle. That Chantilly Lace is like a man magnet. When your future husband hugs you, that fragrance will stick to him, marking him as your territory - private property. Any other woman that comes within a mile of that man will know that he belongs to you. (Scented and dressed like this, won't I also attract other men, Nana?) Easter Beagle, that man will have to fight for your love in order to prove that he deserves you above all others. A good man can handle competition, and will certainly defend his right to claim you as his prize. (Nana, I don't reckon that I want a fighting man.) Listen to your Nana child, else, a hard head will make a soft behind! Don't end up like your momma, manning the fields; bailing the hay; milking the cows; mowing the grass; taking out the trash; and changing the oil on the old blue pickup, after slaughtering hogs in the morn to make sage-seasoned sausage to sell at the market.

(I surely smell something better than Chantilly Lace baking in the oven, Nana.) That is a surprise only for your future husband, Easter Beagle, and that might be him at the front door, knocking. Nana left the kitchen window open so that the aroma floats outside to the porch and fills his nose while he waits for you to greet him at the door; he will fancy a taste of what smells so good.

Are you ready to get, and keep, your man, gal? (Yes, Nana.) Do you have Nana's recipe planted in your head? (Yes, Nana, but I am missing the main ingredient, the sweet potato pie.) Listen to me child; know that you are the main ingredient to Nana's recipe when you leave with that man this evening. If he is truly your future husband, that man will: compliment your smile; gawk at you in that dress; tell you funny jokes; be handsome - and interesting - enough to keep your attention; hold you close while telling you how divinely you smell in Chantilly Lace; sweep your bangs from your brow, while confessing how beautiful you look with a purple orchid in your hair; and, if need be, he will fight to win your heart. Before the end of the night he will proclaim his undying love for you. Then, and only then, should you bring him back home, telling him that you want to thank him for a lovely evening by sharing something special with him. He will think that you plan to give him your body, but you will not, you will be the lady that Nana raised you to be, denying him your womanhood until after you are wed. Child, it is so important that you mind that rule, else you will most certainly end up like your momma, manning the fields; bailing the hay; milking the cows; mowing the grass; taking out the trash; and changing the oil on the old blue pickup, after slaughtering hogs in the morn to make sage-seasoned sausage to sell at the market.

This is a recipe, and all the ingredients are exact. Once you return, and are on the front porch, invite your future husband inside, sit him down at the kitchen at the table, drape a napkin over his lap, walk over to the stove - I'll leave his dessert there. Without telling him that your Nana prepared it, cut him a slice of Nana's special sweet potato pie. Place it in front of him on our best china. Tell your future husband that you love him, seductively gazing into his love-struck eyes while you fork feed the first morsel into his mouth; set the fork down on the table and allow him the choice to finish the remainder of the pie on his own. Before his last

10

bite, your young man will be vexed and begging for more. By this time, next year, that man will be your husband, manning the fields; bailing the hay; milking the cows; mowing the grass; taking out the trash; and changing the oil on the old blue pickup, after slaughtering hogs in the morn to make sage-seasoned sausage to sell at the market - right alongside your grandpa.

'Kind of Blue': A five-part seduction fantasy
By Chris Bell

1. So What (09:22)

So what started this whole thing was when I bought my first copy of 'Kind of Blue' from a woman at the CD store with that slightly quizzical expression animals sometimes have. The loudspeakers in the shop were oozing the irony of Warren Zevon's *Genius*, but she regarded me from the far side of the counter as though she might be interested in what she saw. I watched her flipside closely as she walked away to try and find a CD of pianist Elan Sicroff's 'Journey to Inaccessible Places', a recording consisting of G.I. Gurdjieff and Thomas de Hartmann collaborations. I knew she wouldn't have it; it's been out of print since shortly after it was released.

As she walked away, her backside in those tight jeans looked like two meringues rubbing against one another and I tried to stop myself imagining whipped cream being piped between them.

She looked up the Sicroff on the computer and she was so patient that I was lulled into a false sense of security. After knotting her brows over the database, she told me what I already knew: 'Journey to Inaccessible Places' has been out of print for 19 years. Somehow, coming from her, this was good news.

The following day, after reading about a re-release of 'Kind of Blue' in 5.1 Surroundsound in the latest issue of my favourite audio magazine, I returned to the store with the discounted CD and my receipt and exchanged it for the re-release.

'You realise this one's a Dualdisc? That's why it costs more,' she said, taking my credit card. It felt like a coded message, an invitation. I know, it's tragic; she's a young woman and I'm an old man. But sadly, not only am I old enough to know better, I'm old enough to forget that I know better.

I'm not the spontaneous type, but Miles's spirit of discovery on this record must have inspired me to be more adventurous than usual. Either that or the hangover that had been trailing me all morning had made a yet more irrational person out of me. I banished the mental image of John Coltrane's pensive expression in Don Hunstein's photograph from the 'Kind of Blue' sessions, screwed my clichés to the sticking post and asked her, 'How about dinner?' The question hung on the air like Jimmy Carr's cymbal crash at the beginning of Miles's solo on *So What*.

She put her head on one side, blushed slightly and replied, 'Dinner sounds good.' I was so shocked that I pulled a Celine Dion album out of the bargain bin until I noticed she was staring at its cover, so I jammed it back into the rack.

Her name was Jade, and she was certainly in tune with my new spirit of discovery: her rear-end in tight jeans, the slit up the back of her black top showing a triangle of bare skin, that little animal look. I swung home like a walking bass line, feeling jubilantly blue for the first time in ages — yes, still blue about being old and about life not being as easy as planned, but upbeat nevertheless: a beautiful woman wanted to go out to dinner with me. Somewhere, a far-off football crowd roared.

We dined at a restaurant overlooking the harbour and it went well, except that the vast dining room was so noisy with chat and laughter that I couldn't stay focused on seduction. Somehow, Miles's bravura stayed with me: his band had never done a complete run-through of *So What* in the studio before they recorded the released version.

Throughout our first date Jade had a smile on her face, as though she knew the score and I didn't. 'We should have had dinner at your place,' she shouted. 'I have to keep asking you to say things twice.' I smiled. I didn't mind, and I minded dinner at my place even less. We covered-off the usual conversation topics — work, family, holidays, movies — without getting stuck for something to say. We shared a cab home and I dropped her at her place on the way to mine.

On our second date, the music was the easiest choice of all. It had to be 'Kind of Blue'. Aside from the fact that Jade had sold it to me, it was perfect; ideally suited for seduction — the right length, the right mood, the correct air for me to create an illusion of being cool. Steely Dan's Donald Fagen said its powers of seduction made it "the Barry White of its time".

More ominously, though, the 'Kind of Blue' documentary had some words of warning from Ed Bradley, the Sixty Minutes journalist: if you haven't got over by *Flamenco Sketches* you won't, and she isn't going for your little games. It was a challenge, but I was determined to remain light-hearted. Upon its release, the *Downbeat* magazine review for 'Kind of Blue' said of alto saxophonist Cannonball Adderley that he seemed to be under wraps on all the tracks, "except *Freeloader* when his irrepressible *joie de vivre* bubbles forth". I disagree. To my ears, Cannonball gives Trane a run for his money, to the extent of occasionally aping his phrasing, and his humour shines through as I hoped mine would do, although I'd never tried seducing a woman with jazz.

Jade was due at 20:00. I had my *mise en place* together, onion and garlic peeled and the stock on the boil, and started cooking at ten to eight. When the doorbell rang I was ready. I stood in the doorway clean-shaven and in clean clothes, ushered her in and hung up her coat. Tonight she was wearing her jeans with a dark blue top and she was glowing. She looked better in a pair of jeans than any woman I remembered seeing since 1976. How I knew that and yet couldn't remember what happened last week remains a mystery to me.

The bass and piano intro to *So What* was already playing, so I asked her whose solo she preferred, Trane's or Cannonball's? This was one of my standards, like, "Cary Grant in *North by Northwest* or Humphrey Bogart in *The Big Sleep*?" She said she'd never heard any Miles Davis. I was off to a shaky start and it placed me firmly across from her, leaning forward in my favourite armchair to face her on the sofa. She observed me closely as I marvelled at the curlicue of her top lip.

It was a tentative beginning, but one with integrity: I hadn't struck the right note, but I'd struck it defiantly, as though that was what I'd meant to do.

2. Freddy Freeloader (09:46)

She soon got up and started flicking through old magazines on the coffee table. She seemed cheerful enough and the music made the mood decidedly jaunty, helped, no doubt, by the sheer exuberance of Wynton Kelly's piano. I reckoned the food would be cooked by the end of *All Blues*, so before returning to the kitchen I poured her a glass of the New Zealand Pinot Gris I'd been given by a company for which I did some work last December.

I'd decided on mushroom risotto because it was the only thing I felt confident enough to cook under these nerve-wracking circumstances. Also, the ingredients were all store cupboard staples and, by chance, I had some porcini mushrooms I'd picked up at the deli. As well as the Pinot Gris, there was a bottle of Rioja a friend had left behind.

Even though I was now in familiar surroundings, I felt less confident than I had done at the restaurant, which seemed odd. There was a full moon and I could feel some kind of inner changes going on. Mine's an open-plan apartment, so there was no problem conversing from the stove, but the music started to put me on edge and the cooking wasn't going well. Being a mere male, the multi-tasking required to concentrate on her while stirring was proving a challenge.

'I don't usually like jazz,' she called out. 'It's too… rootley-tootley. Like, the musicians are trying to sound cool.'

She left it at that as Cannonball launched into his tumbling, cascading solo. He sounded pretty cool to me. 'So, what's your verdict on 'Kind of Blue'?' I asked.

'It goes on a bit,' she said, screwing up her nose. Even while pulling a face she looked sexy.

'It's not about the length of the tunes. It's about creating the right atmosphere so the musicians can let go.'

'A bit self-indulgent, isn't it?'

'Well, that depends on your definition of musical excellence.'

'I prefer something more grounded. Rootsier. Fewer notes.'

'I can change the CD if you like.'

'No, it's OK. I need to broaden my horizons and hear something new.'

'Well, 'Kind of Blue' isn't exactly new — it was recorded in 1959.' I reminded myself as I said this that there's no point talking about music; it has to stand for itself.

And yet, by the final coda, as Paul Chambers's bass went into a mini solo of its own, I'd hoisted the flag of optimism and was beginning to watch it flutter atop the mast of sheer exuberance when *Blue in Green* struck up.

3. Blue in Green (05:37)

Jade was a blue-in-green kind of a name if ever there was one. I was just about to make something of that as Miles intoned the opening melody. Without Cannonball, *Blue In Green* is bluer than the other tracks on 'Kind of Blue', and Trane's solo more contemplative.

I was slowly overcome by a mood of missed opportunity, and my risotto was in danger: I'd been distracted from stirring the rice since adding the vermouth and hadn't been ladling in enough vegetable stock. She wanted to chat and the damn stuff stuck to the bottom of the pan while I was listening to the cadences of her voice. My confidence crumbled like the pecorino, but I took the pan off the heat, stirred in some butter, grated in the cheese and let the wounded risotto rest while I re-gathered my troops.

I turned on some mood lighting and she settled back on the sofa. 'So, where do you see yourself in a year's time?' she asked me, sounding suddenly serious and making herself a nest of cushions.

'That's a job interview question, isn't it?'

'Yes, they asked me that one at the shop. I thought I'd see how you coped with it.'

'Well, if it was a work day, I'd see myself on that sofa, watching TV. How about you?'

'I don't look that far into the future. I live in the Now.'

'Very wise. Is that what you told them at the interview?'

'Oh, I think I had that sewn-up by then.'

'If you were dressed the way you are now, I'm not surprised. They'd have been stupid not to hire you.'

'That remark would be considered improper in a job interview…but thanks.'

I thought I detected something imploring in her expression, but I wasn't sure what she wanted from me.

4. All Blues (11:33)

We were going on a journey. I didn't know where we were heading, but I knew what I'd like to be doing when I got there.

I rescued the upper layer of the risotto — thanks to a liberal sprinkling of more grated pecorino — and I don't think any burnt grains of rice sneaked into her portion. I served it in bowls, deciding not to sit at the table but next to her on the sofa, with our knees almost touching.

I was soon in a mood of pastoral reflectiveness. I watched her expression closely as she ate, and her face looked radiant. By the final spoonfuls, night had fallen. The darker mood seemed right for advancement, but somehow I felt constrained by my trite misuse of Miles's masterpiece; the sofa choreography; the stodginess of the risotto. She and the music seemed true to themselves, everything else felt utterly contrived. I tried to step back from myself to reassess the situation. I had abandoned my troops and ridden to the top of a hill, where I was now looking down on the battlefield from above. And yet, things were far from hopeless; there was still a chance of victory. All that was required was a strategy.

I wrung out what was left of my confidence into her glass with the wine. 'Are you trying to get me drunk?' she asked.

'No. I'm trying to get to a place where there's no need for clichés.'
'Sounds a bit pretentious.'

'You're right. I need more wine.' I spilt a little on the coaster but did my best to ignore it. 'Care for some dessert?'

'What did you have in mind?' She seemed to look briefly at my mouth, but I couldn't be sure. Yes and no; plus and minus; dark and light; certain and uncertain; the black and white complementarities of it: one second up, the next second down. Miles knew what he was doing — trilling his closing phrases — but it wasn't rubbing off on me.

I hadn't bothered making a dessert, so I had to use my big move as a diversionary tactic. In for the kill... no, that wasn't right, but this was no time for semantics. There was no other time but *Now* and nothing else but what was in my pants.

5. Flamenco Sketches (09:26)

I sat as close as I needed to in order to be able to put one hand on her thigh. She turned slightly and leaned towards me. Was it my imagination, or were her lips slightly pursed? I hoped her garlic would cancel out mine; there was no time for mouthwash, mints or chewing gum.

Beyond her head, the full moon balanced like a two-dollar coin between the wooden slats of the Venetian blinds and I became aware of the rising and falling of her breathing. When she raised her arms to put them over my shoulders there was a brief but distinct perfume like a vintage Shiraz, followed by something muskier and more feral; sensual, succulent and scented. 'Kiss me,' I said. She hesitated. 'Let's just be ourselves, be brave, skip the formalities,' I pleaded.

She kissed me. It was firm but it was brief, and unmistakeably a once-only, not-to-be repeated sort of kiss. These were very obedient lips. 'Sometimes it's good to be disobedient and just follow your instincts,' I tried.

'You have an interesting way of putting things,' she said as I slid my hand up her thigh. 'And a way of putting things in interesting places.' She looked right at me, but it wasn't the look of the converted. It was the look of the agnostic. And yet the closeness of her face, the touch of her breath…'I think you might have the wrong idea about me,' she said, removing her arms from around my shoulders.

'And what idea is it you think I might have?'

'That I'm easy. I like you, but you're trying too hard. Women don't find that attractive.'

'Hmm.' All right, I had failed. So what?

6. Flamenco Sketches [Alternative Take] (09:32)

My favourite solo on 'Kind of Blue' is Trane's tenor sax on the final track of the re-release. The mood is one of contradictions: a strident lullaby; a tentative flamenco; a happy blues; a blissed-out lament. It called for a different approach to the situation. I was trying to think of one when she said, 'Look, don't take this personally…'

I said, 'I sense a *but* coming and it isn't yours.'

She said, 'Well, perhaps now isn't the right time.'

She got up and pretended to be studying the books on the shelf. It seemed she had found something interesting. She pulled out *Literary Outlaw: The Life and Times of William S. Burroughs*, Ted Morgan's biography, and opened it.

I was talking but I wasn't sure Jade was listening. 'Perhaps I misunderstood. I thought you were interested.'

'I am, but that doesn't mean I'm a pushover. Can I borrow this?'

'I don't lend out books — a bad experience.' She looked at me as though waiting for me to continue. 'A woman I picked up once borrowed my copy of Joseph Campbell's *The Hero With A Thousand Faces* and that was the last I saw of her. How do I know I'll ever see you again?'

'Not a very heroic question. But lend me this and you'll have an excuse to call me.'

'You haven't given me your number.'

'You didn't ask for it.'

I played hurt.

'Don't play hurt. I'd like to see you again and I'd very much like to read this.'

'OK. You can borrow it, as long as you promise not to cut it up.' Jade smiled and sat down next to me on the sofa. Cannonball's alto solo was almost over as my courage retired to an out-of-season resort. When I feebly touched her thigh again she rose, made her apologies and said she had to work in the morning. 'Can I have your number?' I asked.

She didn't answer, just smiled pityingly and made for the door. 'Thanks for dinner, the risotto was nice,' she said.

Kind of blue, and yet, somehow, I could deal with it. At least I'd tried.

Loneliness has its beauty, failure its elegance and hopefulness an occasional, temporary reprise: the following morning, I found a piece of torn paper on the tiles by the front door. On it was scribbled the word "Jade", followed by a phone number.

It took me a week to pluck up the courage to call. When I did, the 'unobtainable' signal laughed at me insistently, translating brilliance into banality, like a computerised travesty of a one-note Miles Davis trill.

Once Upon a Time the Medway Literati
By Lawrence John

Once upon a time, a couple of years ago, the Medway literati consisted of myself and Godknows. I feel this should be known. Just in case you hear it different.

Right the way back, right from when I was small and ever since, I've been cursed with melancholia. The reasons are mine alone so I'll spare you the details, but that particular night - the birth of the literati - I'd decided to end it for good. Sitting on a bench down by the Riverside, I drank to combat the nerves. Within the icy March chill, I went over the slapdash suicide note. Taking in the night view, the settlements and oil refineries - a shimmering lasso around the estuary shore - I psyched myself up for the sleeping pills.

Two hours later I awoke pissed and sprawled upon the frostbitten floor. Cursing to myself that I couldn't do anything right, I was caught between two thoughts: screw the world and down the pills all at once, or scream and toss them into the estuary sludge. I was still considering when I caught sight of something on the horizon. Flashing. Not the usual flashes I knew off by heart, but more a series of flashes, irregular yet patterned, delivered with a burning urgency. With my head still fuggy I watched for a while before realising it was Morse code. Conjuring flashbacks to the Cub Scouts, I quickly pulled a pad and pen from out my satchel. "Hamilton left the door open," went the dots and dashes, "and then he thought better of it and closed it halfway."

And then it stopped. Although I waited a little longer, there was nothing more, just the habitual glittery tints as there had always been, and the sound of water trickling through creaks and inlets. The hollers and chuckles of the marsh birds.

Waking in the afternoon, the events of the previous night consumed the rest of the day. Working it round and round my head I wondered what the message meant. I couldn't let it rest. Close to the time when I had seen the lights before, I ventured down to the river. Sitting at the exact same spot, half expectant, half stupid, I looked out across the water and waited.

At midnight, it began. *"Fall*, by Bill Duncan," the shimmers went, caught between spasms and lethargy. For the next twenty minutes I furiously decoded and read until, "Young voices then a child drawing," signalled the end. I got out my torch and in a beam of fits and spurts, called out across the river, "Who are you."

"Same time tomorrow," came the reply. "Bring along a story."

The following midnight, with all the necessary regalia, Godknows sent me Mike McCormack's *The Gospel of Knives*. When it was done I asked for a name. "Have you brought along a story," came the reply in a flashing cortège. And then, "I do not ask for your name as I have no intention of giving you mine. Do you have a story."

"Riding into Day," I went, "by Beth Nugent." We arranged to make it regular. Same time every night.

For the following month, without fail, we swapped stories from adjacent banks of the Medway. Midnight became the sole purpose of my life and I fell headlong into clock watching. Libraries and bookshops became a mainstay. Half the time I spent browsing; the other half wandering into the eye line of other customers. I was looking for sparks of magic recognition, thinking that every he or she could be Godknows.

Poe, Wilde, Sillitoe, Cheever. Gray, Munro and James Joyce. Anthologies via torch beam coerced into the Medway night. The days became subject to empyrean intrusions. In my imagination I began to conjure images of Godknows and Godknows became a woman. Hemingway, Kafka, Kennedy, Carver. God knows she was beautiful - all my favourite things rolled into one. I gave her starlight skin and nighttime hair. She was speckled with the estuary lights. Babel, Maupassant, McEwan and Borges. She was Medway aurora polaris.

Six weeks passed and the nights were warming with spring. Godknows had just dot-dashed Kelman and while I'd been attentive at the beginning, my mind slipped to other plotlines and conclusions. When a lull in the winking signified the end, I beamed out what I could hold inside no longer. "You are everything. Please. Who are you. What is your name." The reply was immediate. "I have told you. I shall not

21

disclose my name. Please do not ask again." Because Godknows was all I longed for, I didn't care. I sent my yearning skimming across the water. "But what if I want to meet you. What if I want to fall in love with you. I must meet you because you are the one. If I have to I shall swim across." I was about to discard my clothes when Godknows sent a reply. "You will not meet me. Listen. This is important. This is all I ever wanted. To me you are also everything. But believe me, I am hideous. Devoid entirely of any aesthetic favours. I possess penis and breasts, varicose veins and back hair." "Not true," I sent. "Okay," went Godknows. "But within our minds you and I are the people of each other's dreams. Please. Let's not be disappointed. Let's stay beautiful and forever remain that way. We shall not meet. I shall not say my name. Please do not reveal yours. Please be here tomorrow."

I like to imagine that we both sat there in silence. That Godknows also remained there for another hour or so, willing a proclamation, hoping a benediction would relieve the aching repose. That despite what had just been conveyed, Godknows would urge a call of surrender across the ripples of the tide change. But nothing came.

For the whole of the next day I was residual in gloom. Come the evening, the emerging wish-wash of night sky, I was sick with indecision. I wanted to go down to the river, to Godknows, to swap literature via torch-winks. But more than that, I wanted Godknows to be sorry. To want me. I knew the night would be a no show.

The following day felt like forever, by nightfall I was a squall of nerves. I was certain of proposals of love.

Midnight - on the dot - Godknows flashed across the title and author. *The Gift of the Magi* by O, Henry. Once it was done, I was ready to return my own when a new fusion of glows jigged upon the water. "*The Mariner's Tale*," the flashes went. I didn't take any of it down. Consumed with jealousy, as soon as the impostor was done I flashed to Godknows, "What's going on. I thought this was meant to be between me and you." "Where were you last night," was Godknows's reply. Then the alien light shone in, apologising, saying that his name was Don; that he'd been watching, decoding the stories for a week or two. That he'd always wanted to join in, that when I hadn't shown the night before, he'd seized upon the moment. I should have just beamed what I felt then and there, that I wanted him to piss off, that he was intruding on something beautiful. Instead I sent *The Garden Party*. As soon as I had finished, I went home.

The following evening, clinging onto you-never-knows, I ventured once more to the Riverside. I arrived at the spot early, and although it was quiet - no winking lights save for the home-sweet-home habituals - I sensed I wasn't alone. On the off-chance that Godknows was there, I signalled. "Hello. It's me. Are you there. We need to talk." Instantly, from various spots along the estuary shore, fluttered three sets of lights. From the most easterly point came Blake, the most central, Joyce Carol Oates. From the west came recitals of journal entries. Once it stopped, still no beam flickered from Godknows's direction. Not a wink or a spark. I fizzed strobe light obscenities that sizzled upon the water. I wished to blind the world.

I couldn't help it. I continued to frequent the Riverside night after night, probing the panorama for recognition. Godknows continued to evade me, evaded the Medway literati entirely. Week by week, word traversed the length and breadth of the towns and the numbers grew. The estuary at night is now a plethora of fireflies, fireworks and crown jewels, all with a point to prove. Poets, authors and playwrights sparkle new material. Some people flash personal ads, others quote philosophers and movie scenes, song lyrics and bouts of local gossip. I gave up communicating. Instead, unable to pick out Godknows from the rest, I wandered around the perimeter, crossing the bridge at Rochester, sometimes trekking through the tunnel in the hope I might find her. I will never give up. I know she sits there watching. I know that every passing second until we meet will be consumed by dreams of Godknows.

The light show runs continuous, from Upchurch down to Cuxton and back up the river to Hoo St. Werburgh. From there it's on to Grain. Sheerness and Minster complete the circle. Celebrities, movie stars and cultural icons can be seen frequenting the High Streets. The towns are paparazzi heaven.

Once upon a time the Medway literati consisted of myself and Godknows. I just feel it should be known. In case someone tells you different.

The Apple
By Alice Shin

Pant, pant.

Panic and fear dripped from flesh as porous as coffee filters, bitter and acrid and laced with ammonia. A body frozen in the desert heat, muscles stiff and heart pumping twenty pints of blood a minute. Pant, pant. The shovel slipped and clattered onto the solid clay earth, baked rock hard.

Frustration followed when the man realized something below was digging away at the freshly upturned earth.

Pant, pant. Yellow fur. A lolling pink tongue. Digging, digging, digging.

Daniel's hands were raw and his body tired. He picked up his shovel. He was not an animal lover.

'Are you trying to dig something up?' a girl asked. Daniel looked up from the dog and made a note to be more careful. He hadn't noticed her presence until she had opened her mouth. Lucky for her, he was fonder of girls than he was of animals.

She shielded the bright sun from her eyes. 'Judas is really good at digging for things.'

'I don't want him digging for anything, I...' Daniel faltered.

'He can dig for everything and anything. Judas finds all sorts of things all the time – old bones, coins, condoms –'

'Your dog found condoms?' Daniel asked, breaking his gaze. The muscles in his back were sore and the ones in his arms were knotted with fatigue. Perhaps his body needed a little break.

'Oh, yeah – they're not good for him, though, being rubber and everything.' A tilt of the head. An embarrassed smile. 'I'd have to wrestle him so he wouldn't choke on them or anything. Plus, my grandma told me that it's so unhygienic.' She rocked on her heels, her tan face all smiles. 'He even finds all those dead cats and dogs in our backyard, even if they were buried a long way down, he still finds them. He can find everything.'

Daniel pretended to relax with a lean on his shovel, but the knots along his back tightened. Ropes of muscle were pulled taught and threatened to tear. He straightened up and wiped a thin film of sweat from his brow. He gingerly settled on the mound of fresh earth to prevent Judas from making any kind of progress, careful to keep his back straight.

It had taken him hours to make any significant headway. The dry desert sun had baked the ground into a solid mass of soft rock; his spade acted more as a pickaxe than a shovel. He knelt to retrieve his fallen garden tool. 'Sure is hot, little sister.'

'I'm not your sister.'

He tried again. 'Why don't you tell your dog to take a break and start up again when the sun cools down?'

'It's not so hot,' the girl said, but she called her dog to her and took a seat near Daniel. She opened up her knapsack and picked out a bright red apple, so shiny it looked like it was wet with lacquer. 'You want?' she offered.

Daniel shook his head, even though the dry blanket of hot air made him thirsty. Sweat beaded along the sides of his nose and trailed down his face like tears. How long was the girl going to be there? Were her parents nearby? He didn't want to engage the girl in a conversation, but he needed the additional information.

At that moment, he hated the heat, he hated the sun, and he hated his own fatigue. He shouldn't have taken all night to have done what he'd done because now he was forced to interrogate a strange little girl when he wanted nothing more than to be at home in a cool bath, calling in sick.

Not that any of that mattered. For here in the present, there was only the desert, and the sun, and the slow cooking process of his pale skin. By the burn of it, Daniel reckoned that he was the color of that raw, pink pork chop sleeping inside his refrigerator. Stretched out on a Styrofoam plate. Wrapped in plastic. Safe.

'What's your name? How old are you?'

'Me?' she asked. 'Oh, I'll be twelve in a month.'

'That doesn't make you twelve.'

She held it out to him again. A sweet ruby. Nature's jewel. 'You sure you don't want? It's not poison, you know.' Daniel realized that the inside of her wrist was quite pale and what he thought was a tan was actually a fine layer of dirt. The girl had been traveling for a long while. That's when a thought dawned on him. 'So, what are you doing all the way out here?'

She pointed to her dog. 'I was taking him on a walk.'

'Are you...' Daniel was about to say 'lost', but thought the better of it, lest she asked him for a ride. 'You can't get here without a car. How are...Where are your parents?'

Black hair fell over her eyes as she looked down at her red sneakers. Silence hung heavy in the thick heat and Daniel immediately understood, even before she whispered, 'I don't have any parents.' Her voice sounded old. 'Just an alcoholic stepmother and some evil stepsisters.'

'I'm sure they're not that bad,' he said, in hopes that she wouldn't start crying and baring her soul for the next half hour. Daniel wished he were home already because he was both wary and weary. But he didn't have the luxury for the fulfillment of such wishes. And for now, he would have to suck it up and think.

They were half a mile away from the freeway. They were half a mile away from the freeway. He rubbed his face with his free hand to clear his head, but this only served to remind him of his sunburn. It was as though a swarm of wasps had stung his face. His body hurt all over. He wished the girl's body hurt all over. But her skin was a special kind of pale, apparently. The kind that was immune to the ravages of the sun.

The girl pulled her backpack closer to her chest. 'My stepsisters practice black magic satanic stuff. They check out books from the library on it and buy weird knives and plants from eBay all the time. I think they're trying to use it to make some guys take them to the prom or something.'

And there she was, baring her soul. Daniel tried to calculate how much time he would have to devote to her sob story before finding a way to make her disappear. The sun was still high in the sky. Time and the weather were on his side. The heat would keep people from wanting to leave their air-conditioned homes. No one would be aching to take a ride along the dry, cracked freeway that ran along the parched base of cactus-covered mountain. If anything, people were more likely to take a dip in their chlorinated pools than to embark on a picnic in the chemical-free desert.

'Maybe they're misunderstood.'

'No.' She lifted her head, unfazed. 'They're bad.' She took off a red sneaker to inspect the rubbered soles. The girl traced the embossed patterns with her index finger. 'But everyone's bad on the inside, I know.' Her fingers found a shard of glass sticking out of the tan rubber. She plucked it out but pricked her finger in the process. A bead of blood welled up and the girl stuck her finger in her mouth.

Daniel nodded. 'Everyone's bad on the inside,' he repeated. 'That's why God forgives.' A drop of sweat landed on hard clay, was sucked up, and was gone. Like it never was.

'Oh, no,' she said, and stuck her foot back into her red shoe. 'Not always. Sometimes when we know what we're doing is bad and do it anyway – that's worse. And that's when God doesn't forgive.'

'God forgives everybody,' Daniel said, reminding himself not to get heated over an issue with a little girl. 'That's what church is for.' He wished the air wasn't so dry and hot and unforgiving. It only seemed to prove her point, which irritated him further. 'I'm thirsty,' he said. 'You got any water?' He took another swipe at his forehead with the back of his dusty hand. His sweat turned milky at the touch. Poor Daniel felt as though someone had pushed him into a clay oven.

Again, she offered the red apple. 'This'll help. I've got more.'

He accepted the fruit and took a bite. Each munch filled his mouth with cool, sweet juice. Maybe all Daniel needed was a crunchy, Washington red apple to occupy him for the next few minutes, so that he could figure out what his next move would be. The girl seemed occupied herself, hunched over a spiral-bound notebook.

Her long, silver pen flashed dangerously in the light of the sun. Its reflections bounced off into Daniel's eyes and pierced his vision like glass. He blocked the bright flashes of sun with his hand, still devouring the sweet red apple.

How long had it been since he'd eaten? All he had cared about for the past four hours was digging and burying, but now that he was forced to sit down and eat, he was ravenous. He ate it down to its core, eating every bit of its skin. Still hungry, he ate the very core itself. And when he was done, he asked for more.

The girl gave her apples to him freely and he pounced on each new offering, ravenous. Now that he'd thought about it, he'd gone sixteen hours without food of any sort. He couldn't consume them quick enough, gnawing at the core as though he were a wolf at a bone, crunching on the seeds as though they were nuts. What he needed was a meat and potatoes meal from the nearest Denny's, but all the girl seemed to have were apples. He took what he could get, trying to fill the insatiable pit in his stomach. The silver stem she was writing with continued to flash in his face, which made his head ache. Still, he didn't complain because he was still hungry and wanted more apples.

He knew that he should be thinking about what his next move would be, but he wasn't done devouring. He couldn't think until his hunger had subsided, so he continued to crunch and munch and slurp and gnaw, downing one after the other, too consumed to taste anything anymore.

And then they were gone.

'Look it,' she said, and turned her backpack upside down. She shook it in a show of demonstration. 'I don't have anymore. You sure are hungry, aren't you?'

She put her notebook away and Daniel was glad that her pen was put to rest, too, jammed into the back of her jeans. But the relief was short lived. The sun had over ripened to a deep orange, hanging low and quiet in the sky. It was ready to go to sleep and the subsequent rush-hour traffic would be pulling all those cars back onto the roads, all those people in offices who would be rushing to get back to their air-conditioned homes, havens in which they could disengage from actual people and re-entangle themselves with the versions of real people on TV – some, in high-definition.

'Isn't your stepmother going to be worried?' Daniel asked, a little spent, but with a dark impatience that grew at the corners of his thoughts. And each thought multiplied like mildew.

He didn't have any more time for her. People would be on their way back home. Some might pull over to take a short piss because the bathrooms at the office were backed up. Because they didn't feel like pissing in a McDonald's bathroom aglow with artificial light. Because it would be so much more convenient than pulling up to a dirty gas station. Because God seemed to have forsaken him at the moment.

And some of those people might wander a little bit too far into the desert, in search of some privacy, some brush or garden of cacti.

'Don't you have to get back to her? Where is she?' He tried to sound calm, even as his fingers curled themselves around his shovel.

'I ran away a long time ago,' the girl said. 'She's stopped pretending to look for me, so I'm olly-olly-oxen free.'

The sight of the slipping sun made Daniel's heart beat all the faster. He got to his feet. The steel head of the shovel scraped against rough clay. 'You've got to go, little girl. And your dog – '

The dog had unearthed half of his morning's work, much to Daniel's distress. All those hours of fighting with unyielding desert clay. The desire in his quivering muscles to give in to fatigue. Daniel wanted to cry. 'Tell your damn dog to get the hell out of here!'

The dog lifted its head with a growl. Its bared teeth reminded him of the wolves he had seen on the Discovery Channel, their eyes glowing and burning into the cameras, unafraid. Daniel's heart convulsed, sick with the dog's betrayal. Wasn't Judas supposed to be a man's best friend? His breath came fast and he got dizzy. It would take at least another hour to redo what the dog had undone and another five minutes to get the girl and the dog the hell out of there.

'Hey, Daniel,' the girl said, standing. 'You ate all my apples.'

'Yeah,' he said, breathing as though he'd just run a marathon, 'I'm sorry. Tell you what, I'll give you twenty bucks if you and your dog get on out of here right now and get yourself some dinner.' The cars. He could have sworn he heard the cars. 'Hell, I'll give you forty, maybe you can catch a cab back home. It's not fun being all alone on the road all the time.'

'No, that's okay.'

The sky burned red as the sun touched the horizon. His hourglass was about to run out. Daniel lifted a shovel that felt twenty pounds heavier than it should have.

'Did you know that apple seeds have cyanide in them?' she asked, taking a step towards him.

'What?'

'But it's in such a small amount that you'd have to eat a whole bushel of apples to die or anything,' she mused.

The air was cool on his flesh, but Daniel was still sweating. She was right. He had eaten all her apples. The head of the shovel jammed into the earth and held him steady. 'I never told you my name,' he breathed. The dizziness spiraled into an ever-expanding vortex. He lost his grip. The spade clattered on cracked clay.

'You didn't have to.'

He was on his knees. 'But I don't know yours.'

'Of course, you wouldn't,' she said, indulgent. 'But right now, I've got to wake someone up. You understand, right?'

Daniel was on all fours, dripping and nauseous.

'Don't you worry about a thing, Daniel. When you go to sleep, you can take her place,' she said, soothing. And though Daniel was still breathing and very much alive, the end to his story had already been written in a flash of silver – by the time the desert sun would rise again, his body, fragrant with bitter almond and apples, would be left to bake in the depths of the parched earth. 'You know,' she continued, taking a seat next to him, 'I always thought that God doesn't forgive everybody. But why don't you go see and find out?' she asked.

As Daniel lay on the dry terrain, each of its cracks thirsty to slake itself with his dripping sweat, a series of convulsions attacked his body. But the girl was too occupied helping Judas unearth the sleeping beauty to watch the show. It did, however, remind her of a time, long ago, when someone was forced to wear a pair of iron sandals, red-hot, and dance herself to death at someone's wedding. Or was that a just a little bit of dream mixed in with an old story? The girl couldn't remember.

The last of the dirt was removed and as it turned out, Daniel had wrapped a girl's body in plastic. The girl reached for her silver pen, its smooth surface glinting in the light of the moon. She used it to slice through several layers of garbage bags to reveal the face of a woman.

Outside the edge of the pit, Daniel gave a final thrash and lay still forever. The girl leaned over, and kissed her.

City Limits
By Meleina Backhaus

She snuck out of her bed every night for five years.

The first time had been so exciting her hands shook. Now, it is a practiced routine. She waits until her husband is asleep, slides out of bed and puts on jeans and a t-shirt; sweater if it's cold. She moves quickly and quietly down the steps, out the door and into the garage; keys always on the top shelf by her watering can.

Her fathers 59' Buick is too big to fit into the garage, so parking on the street is necessary. Once she hits the edge of her neighborhood it's smooth coasting down the hill, picking up speed, sailing through the light flashing yellow after midnight.

Two more lights wink at her as she picks up speed, so that by the time she's in the industrial district she's doing ninety. Lights fade and give way to darker patches of fields; blanched bunches of grass spotlighted by her headlights clinging stubbornly to the road.

Then darkness, then a single light up ahead marking the end of her flight.

The city limit sign, with its town name, population and welcome, is highlighted by a large fluorescent yellow bulb that buzzes with mosquitoes in summer and is tinged with frost in winter.

Next to it – a run down bar where pick-up trucks jockey for space and music thumps against the windows. The owner's black and orange striped jeep always anchored to the corner of the porch.

She'd never been there, had never been past the sign. She couldn't go past it, couldn't bear to watch possibilities turn into responsibilities. So she slowed down, her headlights reaching into the dark where she was afraid to go.

She always drives the speed limit when she goes back.

*

He could always tell it was her; the headlights were unmistakable. Christ, who drove a Buick that old anyway? He would never have even known it was a *she* if summer evenings didn't last so long. Whenever she slowed down it was like an old movie; her fair hair blowing in the wind making her neck long and graceful.

Most nights he had to peer through a haze of smoke, the smell of booze and all the rough sounds that came with a bar, to see the twin beams coasting down the highway. That car was hard to miss. It made him think of drag racing and cigarettes and real rock music; and he had to admire a woman who wasn't afraid to open up that beast of an engine and let it ride.

He also respected a woman who had so much self-control.

All the women he knew did what they wanted when they wanted, and usually never realized that they'd been talked into what they wanted. They wore too tight tank tops and jeans that were made to fit a twelve year old. Their hair was frizzy and dyed and their makeup was loud. They were fun and boisterous and lazy and crazy and mostly just as fucked up as all the losers they slept with.

She never went past the sign - not in the six years he'd come to expect seeing her headlights late at night - coming up fast, then slowing down to a crawl, then sitting on the sign for exactly five heartbeats, before she turned around and went home.

His life was washing glasses and popping beer tops and fixing backed up toilets and rebuilding transmissions. He tended bar until two in the morning and chased away the same old drunks. He had all the freedom and excitement a guy in a fairly small town could ask for.

When she drove by, time slowed down for a minute and he could imagine a life where he wasn't busting his ass to break even - drank microbrew beers instead of domestic and then sat out on his stained mahogany deck to watch his grass grow. It was always a nice quiet moment until someone interrupted it, yelling for another round of shots, or puking on the bar, or two guys trying to kill each other; then it was back to business as usual, muscling people around and smiling and listing to everyone's bullshit.

They saw a bartender; rough, quick tongue and easy smile and hell-of-a-right-hook-if-need-be; they didn't see the guy who wanted some peace and quiet. He imagined that's where she came from. A place full of quiet and peace and order; and if he was honest with himself, he knew that's what she pretended to run away from every night.

Sometimes he went to bed thinking about her, imagining she picked him up at the city limit sign and they coasted into the dark with only the faint red trail of two taillights to mark their escape.

Instead he dreamed the truth; that someday she might get out of her car and walk past the sign to pick a wildflower out of the ditch and breathe in the air. She would turn and see him outside the bar, in front of the windows, watching her.

He would wave and she would smile; then she would drive away and he would walk back inside, and they would both be old.

So Very Necessary
By Stacy Taylor

The pill bottles have fallen over. Tiny pink tablets spill into the sink, vanishing down the drain before my slow fingers can stop them. Rowena watches. Her face not quite blank. I watch, too, unsure about what to do. The pills are so very necessary.

I remember when the first full bottle came here, how afraid we were. How wary about the changes the pills it contained might bring. We put them in the medicine cabinet and discussed how we would make them an orderly part of our orderly lives. Now, they are as necessary as food and water.

Rowena is a waif, a sylph, a vague thin shape in green cotton panties. Her face is too white, too thin, too expressionless, and all I can do is lead her to her favorite rocking chair while I fret inside about the pills.

'Thank you, Roger.'

'Love, I'm not Roger.'

'I'm not love.'

We lock eyes for a moment, then I get her a glass of water before I search the cupboards for more pills. She rocks quietly, not seeing me, dark messy hair hiding her skinny cheekbones, harsh ceiling light painting phantoms along her rib cage like a shadowy ghost-ladder against a white padded wall.

We laughed in Old Montreal once; I remember it well: the boutiques, the street musicians, Old Montreal Port, the architecture, and *Chez Queux* restaurant where we agreed to finally marry. How giddy she was, how happy to be alive. I remember laughing at everything, especially each other.

We don't go out now. She takes her clothes off because she can't stand fabric against her skin. She will disrobe wherever the spirit moves her: Restaurants, markets, hardware stores. Her face is placid when she does this, her heart innocent, but shoppers with small children don't like it. I don't like it, either. Men stare at her with lustful eyes and lewd smiles, even though she's thin, and women say cruel things about her behind their hands. Sometimes, the police are called.

So, I keep her at home, where there are always pills, unless they tumble down the drain.

'Randy, will you sit with me?'

'I'm not Randy, darling. I need to find the pills.'

'I know.' And when she smiles--such a child--light shines from her and turns my knees to jelly. 'You're not Randy, you're Raphael. You came to me in a dream. I invited you to stay. You did. Remember?'

'Rowena ---'

'I'm not Rowena. Call me Jade,' she says, softly. 'I so love Jade.'

I nod and search the cabinet over the refrigerator, moving aside bug dope and sixty-watt bulbs. Rowena begins to hum. In her voice, I hear magic and music and so much elusive laughter. I come across the spare fuses I couldn't find last fall when Rowena shorted out her hair dryer. I'd had no choice but to hide it from her after that, which broke my heart, but she'd left it running for hours, dancing naked in the warm bathroom.

I quit my job shortly thereafter.

There are no pills in the cabinet over the refrigerator. Why must they be so very necessary?

When I turn back to her, there is a blue plastic hairbrush sticking from her body in the place where green panties were a moment before. The black bristles look so dark beside her white skin; she is ecstatic, thrusting. Oblivious.

I watch, and I don't know if I should. I begin to harden, and I don't think I should. But I can't stop watching her. Her expression, usually so bland, enchants me.

Rowena puts things inside herself because she hungers for pleasure, but she can't bear to touch her own skin, and I, weak creature that I am, can't take my eyes away from her.

She moves slowly at first, perhaps without joy, but her brown eyes begin to shine, her body tenses, and she climaxes hard. Staggering, I go to her on legs that barely support me and put my head near her lap, careful not to touch without approval, inhaling her sweetness.

'Ronald,' she says, 'can we do it? Is it all right?'

'Yes, honey, if that's what you want. But I'm not Ronald, and what about the pills?'

'I know, and I'm not Jade now. I'll be Ruby for a while. The letter is right, isn't it, Romeo? R?'

I nod, my eyes wet, and I think about how I should find the pills. Almost coquettish now--helpless, hungry, hazy--the look in her eyes makes me forget pills. For a moment, anyway.

Only when I am inside her, can I believe it is as it should be, but even then, it is clearly not. She lies in the chair unmoving, the only clue to her pleasure the disconnected rhythm of her breath against my throat and the brace of her body urging me to hurry. I feel her sharp bones beneath me. Her helplessness. Her breakability. These are the only times I'm allowed to be this close to her. She endures for the pleasure; she forgets she must endure *because* of the pleasure.

I grasp her hips carefully, pull her to the edge of the seat, and slip inside. The passage is exquisite. She gasps, bottom lip clenched between tiny white teeth, her fingernails scratching at the finish on the rocker. And me? I am encased in the tightest sheath, friction undefined already working against me, sucking me deeper into the chasm that is her, Rowena. I want to die inside her; I want to be here forever.

I'm crying, and fucking, and loving, and her gentle mewls are guttural groans. Very slightly, so slight that it's difficult to be sure, she moves from the inside out. Clutching, releasing, sucking, relaxing--her small hips working, her nearly concave belly rippling like a dancer, and me, drowning in her feel, her smell, her heat, her utter unreachableness.

She feels *this*, goddamn it. She fucking feels *this*. She feels *this* ... *this* ... feels it ... she fucking *feels* ...

Lost, found, confused, I try to kiss her but she jerks away as though I am diseased and, well, maybe I am. The sudden despair in my voice is louder than her moans, but I fuck her hard anyway, helpless against the way I feel. I haven't kissed her lips for so long, but I can remember exactly how sweet she is.

Spin up . . . spiral down . . . almost there . . . almost.

I'm surprised when she comes because she touches me. Sometimes Rowena forgets she hates skin and grabs me with both hands, hissing between clenched teeth, pulling me closer. Like right now.

Oh my God, oh my God, so good.

In a world without touch, this moment eclipses my orgasm, just her small hands on my bare skin. Ejaculation continues, regardless, but my elation lies elsewhere, rejoicing in bony fingers scrabbling at my arms and neck, and a pretty face whose paleness is eaten by color.

I'm still now, spent and ashamed, my head against her chest as she catches her breath. And I weep, knowing that once again I couldn't fuck it all away for her. The valleys between each of her ribs are so deep that pools form if I cry for long. I try not to, because it disturbs me, and she doesn't like to see me cry. Impatient to be left alone again, she squirms. I pull out, reluctantly, letting my fingertips trail the softness of her thigh in order to absorb the last feel of her into my skin.

My beautiful baby.

A warm wet cloth is about all she can take against flesh that just felt so much so fast, and I clean her gently before I resume my search for pills. Her eyes have less of that faraway look but she still sits naked and mute, tapping a song from the 70s, "Billy, Don't be a Hero," I think, onto the wood of the rocking chair.

I cannot find the pills, and it is bedtime, so I lead her to our room. She lies down on her special flannel sheets and curls into a tangled abstract. I notice gooseflesh along her arms and turn up the furnace, and then I slip in beside her.

'Goodnight, Rodney,' she says.

'Goodnight, Rowena.'

'Not Rowena ... someone else ... whoever you want me to be.'

I just want her to be Rowena.

Where are those fucking pills?

Rowena used to be bigger, her beautiful body curvy and soft. I used to be bigger, too, in many ways, but the years have taken their toll. I think about our honeymoon, two weeks in a cabin near Wasilla, two blissful weeks of fucking in the snow, stewed wild rabbit, a fireplace, and oh dear God, Rowena's giggle. There were no pink pills.

I don't know whom the pills are for. The doctor says they are so very necessary, but when darkness covers the house and Rowena breathes deep beside me, I wonder.

I want to hurry into sleep because I'm afraid of the interim; I will my eyes still and regulate my heartbeat. There is peace, and Rowena's steady breathing lulls me.

A sound nearby, a rustle, brings me back. I sense a shape by the bed, or perhaps it is a waking dream. Unsure, I try to pull my eyes away from sleep's grasp. It is Rowena and she is not naked. She is beautiful, soft and curvy, in flannel pajamas printed with lavender flowers.

A name falls from her lips, 'Robert.' It is I; I am Robert. She tries to stroke my forehead, but her hand slides through me and touches only a cold pillow. My heart beats faster, faster, and I'm shivering through a wave of chills as I sweat out my fear.

Sleep quietly reaches for me, intent on its purpose.

My eyes are opening, closing, and opening again. Through leaden lids, I see a bottle on my night stand. Maybe I've found them at last. The bottle has fallen over and is empty, a cap by its side, and right before I slip into total, dead sleep, I notice the name on the label. The room is dark, I can't be sure, but I think I see an R and an O and is that a --?

Rowena is crying; I hear her. She says my name, Robert, again and again and again.

The pills. They're so very necessary.

Blue Flowers

By T. Rigney

Blue flowers, every four hours.

Instructions on paper. Clean script; borderline perfection.

A sickness, it read. And this is the only cure.

Chad picks a petal and opens her mouth, places it carefully on her tongue. Brings the cup of water to her mouth and tips it forward. The petal swims, floats, and disappears down her throat. He pushes her mouth closed and watches her sleep.

The book he's reading is long, the print small. He adjusts his spectacles and squints. Chad needs better glasses, a stronger prescription. The words are blurry; they seem to swarm the page in search of purpose. He squints harder.

Headache sets in. Pops an aspirin to ease the pain.

Cell phone rings. He answers it.

'Hello?' he asks.

A female voice. Sweet, kind of bitter. 'What's up?'

He says, 'Not much. Reading and caring for my client.'

'Isn't that weird?' the voice wonders.

'Is what weird?'

'Your job.' She means Maria. She means the blue flowers. Every four hours.

'It's weird,' he admits. 'No weirder than dancing for money.'

The voice is silent. He's touched a nerve.

'You opened the door,' he adds.

'You didn't have to go there,' she tells him.

'Well, don't open the door.' He stands firm. Fuck her feelings. Fuck her.

'Why did you call?' he asks.

'I miss you,' she says after a moment.

'You can come see me anytime you want,' he tells her.

'It's weird,' she confesses. 'You sitting beside that woman, feeding her flowers. It's just weird, you know? I couldn't handle it.'

'You could,' he says. 'If you really wanted to see me.'

'Go to hell,' she spits. 'And you could've come see me at work if you wanted. Until you just up and disappeared, of course.'

'It gets old,' he says, pinching the bridge of his nose. She's making the headache worse. Pops another aspirin, downs it with coffee. 'You know? It gets old watching your girlfriend dance naked in front of horny men. Drunk men. Men who should be at home fucking their wives.'

'It's temporary,' she says, trailing off.

'It's been four years,' he sighs. 'Temporary? More like career.'

'Go to hell,' she says again. This time it's followed by an electronic beep.

The cell phone lists the details of the call. Five minutes, thirty seconds.

A new record.

The confrontation has left him edgy, manic. The sentences dance away from the page and the book sails across the room. Chad is on his feet, huffing, his fists threatening violence to anything, anyone. Book hits shelf, lamp hits floor.

Shatters into pieces.

Fitting.

Living here, in this house, in the next room to this woman who never wakes, was supposed to be for the better. He would learn to appreciate his lady, and she would learn to appreciate him. But it's driven a stake between them, slicing their relationship into wedges like birthday cake. These calls were supposed to be pleasant. Now he dreads the ring-ring-ring of the phone.

It, too, flies across the room.

It, too, connects with the shelf.

Shattering into fragments of circuitry that serve no purpose in such a state.

'No!' he shouts. 'You go to hell!'

Infuriated, he throws himself into the recliner next to the bed. Sets the alarm for seven o'clock, just in time for another dose.

Of blue flowers.

In just under four hours.

*

Seven o'clock the alarm sounds.

Buzz, buzz, buzz.

He sits up suddenly. Rubs his eyes.

Every four hours, like clockwork. The routine is always the same.

Chad picks a petal and opens her mouth, places it carefully on her tongue. Brings the cup of water to her mouth and tips it forward. The petal swims, floats, and disappears down her throat. He pushes her mouth closed and watches her sleep.

Spots the busted phone on the floor. Broken into pieces. He walks over and collects them. His phone, his favorite thing. Shattered.

Fitting.

He sits in the recliner and tries to put it back together again. Even Humpty Dumpty would have to laugh. Wires protrude, metal bends. Battery in place, he presses the plastic cover into its groove. Presses the power button. Signal - three bars strong. Then it dies.

Wires protrude, metal bends.

Battery in place, he repeats the process.

Signal - three bars strong.

Then it dies.

'Great,' he says, head in hands. 'Just great.' He lets the phone fall to the floor, where it returns to chaos. 'Just fucking great.'

There's no phone in this house. No electronic devices of any kind, minus the clock. It's a Victorian nightmare, all pinks and greens and off-whites. Trapped in glass, carved in wood, then forgotten. He has no way of making amends. No way of professing his sorrow to her, his disdain for himself. Words come easy when no ears can hear them.

Leaving is not an option; his hometown is over two hours away.

Never make it back for the dosage.

Losing this job is not an option. The afternoon conversation has surely left him homeless. He imagines her throwing his meager belongings out the bedroom window. A screwball comedy without the zany humor, without the happy ending and the swelling music. Just a pile of useless things on the sidewalk.

Inside, a girl with a broken heart.

This is home now. This is his life.

These blue flowers.

These hollow hours that come in fours.

*

In the pantry, sorrow in a bottle.

One shot, then two.

Fuck it.

Eight or nine in a row.

Fuck it all.

Staggering, he ventures through the mansion. Room after room of antiques, pretty things in frames. He smiles in a gigantic mirror, tries on a coat older than his grandfather. He spins a globe crafted before the Civil War, walks in shoes worn by a slave. He touches things that have not been touched in decades. He cries in a chair made of velvet.

Alcohol in the bloodstream, head full of regret.

He says things to the air, confesses secrets to the walls. There was a time when words came so freely that he wondered if they would cost him in the long run. Thoughts were clearer then, intentions and emotions not one and the same. He tells her that he loves her, tells her he wants to take her away from all the bad stuff in the world. No more neon, no more bounced checks. He doesn't want to say awful things that sting, that cut worse than weapons ever could.

He watches his feet as he loses balance.

Connects with the floor.

The pain makes him laugh. The loose tooth makes him grimace.

The blood flows from split lips as he watches the room tumble and twirl, tumble and twirl.

Alcohol in the blood stream, head full of forget.

About things like Maria.

About things like blue flowers.

That must be administered every four hours.

*

He sits up suddenly. Rubs his eyes.

Oh, no. No, no, no.

'No,' he says. It was night just moments ago; now daylight penetrates ancient curtains, casting dull light on duller objects. The place has lost its charm; these thick walls and high ceilings conceal a series of rooms full of things collected by faceless employers who promise big rewards.

Once the job is finished.

But not now. These thoughts are unimportant.

'No,' he says again. 'Oh, God. No!'

Groggy, head swimming, he stumbles through the halls.

This way?

No, this way.

Knocks over an urn, ashes spill. Bumps a table, books fall. Then he's in her room, tripping over an area rug and grasping madly for the petals.

The blue flowers.

But four hours has turned into eight, which has turned into twelve.

Three doses missed.

And she's awake, her eyes open, her body seemingly frozen to the mattress. She hasn't even uncovered herself; the heavy comforter still masks her figure, her dimensions. Chad falls to his knees at her bedside and places his forehead against her arm.

'I'm sorry,' he says. 'The blue flowers. I'm so sorry.'

'Please,' she manages to say.

'I can't do anything right,' he sobs. 'I can't even do this right. I'm a total failure. A phony. A guy who thinks the future doesn't apply to him.'

'Please,' she manages to say.

'I'm sorry. You must be in pain.' Ignoring her eyes, he plucks a petal from the plant. Takes the glass of water.

But she's looking at him. Intensely.

He moves to her mouth, but then she speaks.

'Please,' she says slowly, softly. 'Please. The blue flowers.'

'Every four hours,' he cries.

'Yes,' she says. 'Feed me the flowers. They keep me here. Every four hours I start to stir; I can feel my dreams thinning. Every four hours I feel it on my tongue, and I go away again.' She speaks in sputters, a cheap engine fighting winter wind. 'Feed me the flowers.'

'Why?' Chad asks. 'What is all of this?'

'I hear everything,' she says, eyes flooded with fear. 'I know what he wants. This mansion, this house - it's a meat locker. A feeding trough.'

He cocks his head, confused. A puppy discovering the world around him.

'You sedate, he feeds,' she explains slowly, her voice raspy. 'I hear everything. I know his system. I know what he's capable of.'

'I'll get you out of here,' Chad says. He stands and wipes his face. 'I'll save you.'

'He'll find us,' Maria tells him. 'He always does.'

'But -'

'I know what he's capable of,' she says. 'You're dead if you leave here with me.'

'Then what do we do?' Chad wants to know.

Maria sighs. 'Feed me blue flowers, every four hours.'

'But – '

'Feed me blue flowers, every four hours. I've come to terms with this. So should you.'

It makes no sense. He can't grasp it.

Chad shakes his head. 'No. I can't let this happen. I can't, can I? I can't let this happen. I can't fail you, too.'

She meets his eyes with her own. 'Listen to me. I'm okay with this. I've made my peace. Don't let him destroy you, too.'

'But -'

'Blue flowers, every four hours.' Then she opens her mouth.

'I'm sorry,' he says, throwing up his hands. The petal falls to the floor. 'I can't.'

'Give me the flowers. Collect your reward.' She meets his eyes with her own. 'Fix your life. Put things in order. Because you can't stop this. No one ever has. There will be more after me, more after you. It's a cycle, unbroken and strong. So let me help you set things straight.

'For you.'

'How do you know about me?' he wonders.

'I hear everything,' she says with a sad smile.

'This is wrong. It's not right. If I warm up the car, we can be in town _'

She just shakes her head. 'Blue flowers.'

'Every four hours,' Chad finishes.

He meets her eyes with his own.

And they understand each other perfectly.

He leans forward, kisses her forehead gently. Four sets of tears fall.

Chad picks a petal and opens her mouth, places it carefully on her tongue. Brings the cup of water to her mouth and tips it forward. The petal swims, floats, and disappears down her throat. He pushes her mouth closed and watches her sleep.

It's a process, a mechanical act. He tells himself this so he won't feel.

In three weeks he'll rebuild, restart. Put his life back in order.

Until then, he'll respect her wishes.

With blue flowers.

Every four hours.

Baptisms

By Teri Davis Rouvelas

Morgan is playing motorboat with her baby, Alexa. Brrrr brrrr. She pulls Alexa through the deep waters of the swimming pool by her tiny hands. Brrrr brrrr. Alexa laughs her braying laugh, water curlicuing over a twisted back, sunlight gleaming off the silvery strands of very thin hair. Morgan smiles. It's her private time with Alexa. Her other daughters - Linny and Hella - are inside napping, sucking twin thumbs, dreaming twin dreams.

Brrrr brrrr. Morgan releases her baby's hands and watches as Alexa slips beneath the surface, still laughing. Her lopsided grin can be seen all the way to the bottom of the pool, where she rests and waits until their next special, private time.

*

Gray eyes haunt Morgan from cupboards as she makes gazpacho from leftover salad. She reaches for a pepper mill and almost impales one with a long, shell-pink fingernail. Trying to ignore the eyes, she grinds and grinds until the mill falls into the soup from wilting hands. She twists slightly and bends in half as if searching for a contact lens on the floor.

Tears roll down her face, but this could be from the chopped onions. Or maybe she inadvertently touched her lashes with a Tabasco-dipped finger. Linny, who is five-going-on-six, stands in the doorway and motions to Hella, who joins her to gape at their mother.

Hella starts sucking her thumb, a habit stopped one year ago - except when sleeping - and picked up again like smoking. Just one suck - what harm can it do? Drool slides down her thumb and onto the front of her mermaid queen t-shirt. Linny joins her twin in outgrown baby habits and lightly wets her pants.

Their mother straightens up, sees them, and smiles. Her babies are back. The tears were for all of them, but despite the ache in her chest, she tells herself she was crying because of the onions. She must always tell herself that.

Morgan walks over, kneels and gathers her damp twins in her arms. They weep in frightened, well-conditioned silence while she murmurs a nursery rhyme song as, one by one, she pulls out a few strands of hair from their scalps to weave around her empty ring finger later. She wants remembrances of this moment; she wants to marry this moment. Her babies are back in her arms, sitting on her thighs, no longer half-grown children but infants again.

The twins stare at each other and say nothing. Linny's urine seeps through Morgan's sweatpants. They don't notice, nor do they notice the wetness that hangs like a bib around Hella's neck.

Their mother hungers for her own clone. She wants to see what it's like to be an identical twin, to have another who looks exactly like her. At times, she wants to reverse the process of birth and bring her babies back up and inside her where they'll be safe. Instead, she releases the twins, claps her hands and instructs them to change their clothing, wash up, Daddy may be on his way home.

They race upstairs towards their shared bedroom, then slow down and tiptoe by the closed door of the nursery, not wishing to wake Alexa. She's been taking a nap for ages. They don't want her to cry again because Daddy may be on his way home, and he's been at work for a very long time.

Everything's been very different for a while - maybe as long as they've been five-going-on-six. Certainly as long as Alexa's been sleeping. The twins can't quite remember. They only know one stinks almost constantly of concentrated urine, and the other is getting a blister on her thumb. Morgan listens to the movements upstairs and finishes the gazpacho with a squeeze of lemon juice before throwing it against the wall. Blood drips, scatters, puddles, but it's not blood any longer than a brief moment. It's tomato juice and bits of pureed vegetables; it's leftover salad, and it isn't on the wall anymore. That would be wasteful, and her husband Mark may get angry.

No, not Mark. Mark isn't her husband. Mark is the man who comes over on Fridays. Her husband is ... someone else. She tries to remember his name as she ladles a bowl of soup.

Brrrr brrrr. She hears herself outside playing with Alexa. It's their private time, but the baby isn't laughing. How can she? Mommy isn't with her; it's someone else. It's a sham Mommy, a stranger Mommy. Alexa can tell the difference.

Good, Morgan thinks, she knows her mommy, who loves her.

Morgan starts to eat her soup. She smells faintly of urine and onions but not tears; she can never smell of tears. Roy will leave her again. Now, she remembers: her husband is Roy, not Mark. Mark is the man who rapes her every Friday. More men would love to come over and take her by force because Morgan is beautiful. All men who see her want her; all women who see her hate her, especially the ones with eyes shadowed like hexes and who once had to pretend worn, thready bath towels were long, blond hair - hair she has naturally.

Morgan is very beautiful and hated by most people because there are more women in the world than men. She doesn't care. She knows the game and has for a long time. It's a game with rules, and she knows each rule very well. They helped her lawyer let ten men with hooded, shifting eyes and two women with long, blond hair see the reality of Morgan, the lovely and loving mother.

Now, the twins' footsteps are descending the stairs, so their mother screams, "Go take a nap!" The footsteps hurry in retreat. A hushed door closes.

She wants her private time with Alexa. And then, it will be Friday night; Mark will be here.

Brrrr brrrr. The bowl of soup slips from her hand and smashes into pieces. She leaves the kitchen to run outside, but it's too late. Alexa has returned to the bottom again, and she's grinning her lopsided smile. Her first and only baby tooth flashes white under the water. Morgan frowns down at her, but Alexa keeps smiling up towards her mommy. Alexa crinkles her gray eyes into slits until she looks almost fetus-like - a fetus returned to her amniotic world.

Morgan is glad to be out of the kitchen and away from gray eyes hiding in cupboards because she hates when they don't blink. She smells of onions and urine. Naked, she still smells of onions and urine. She enters the pool and waits.

*

Upstairs, the twins are finally sleeping again. Once more, they've gone to bed hungry. Hella hears the dim sounds of the pool in her sleep and she wets her pants this time. Urine flows from her like the water which continually flows over Alexa - Alexa, now gazing up as her mother moans into bubbles that emerge from full, pink lips and pop in silence on the surface while the twins sleep on.

Morgan stares down through the water at Alexa, who waits at the bottom of the pool. She wants her daughter to see what men do to her - these men who think she's so beautiful - and know Morgan can never *not* be beautiful or desired. Alexa is ugly and will never have men wanting her. Morgan watches the baby watching her, watching Mark, watching what they do. He grunts, pushes and then shivers, his hands clenching her hips to his, his breath hot on her spine. The rape of her body is over. All that's left is the rape of her mind.

And he tries to rape her mind by turning her around to kiss her, and she closes her mouth to his tongue.

The twins sleep on in the room next to the nursery, the one where Alexa naps. They've never played motorboat with their mother. That's Alexa's game - ugly, little Alexa with her bug-like gray eyes and a crooked grin to match a crooked back, Alexa, who loved to float in her ridiculous duck-headed ring and splash her stubby arms, kick her stumpy legs.

Then, she would cry because she couldn't tell Mommy if she was hungry or scared or tired. Alexa screamed, and she was even uglier when she cried.

Daddy hates crying (Linny recalls this in dreams), but he hates Alexa's silence more. Mommy likes the silence. Linny dreams of the

53

bright orange duck ring bobbing empty. A dark shape rests on the bottom of the pool, rocking gently back and forth as Mommy emerges from the water, sees Linny staring and runs towards her, screaming to take a nap, go finish your nap, what are you doing looking at me all the time.

This dream rests on the first day Linny, awake, began wetting her pants again. Hella's thumb was lodged in her mouth as Linny ran past her, and Mommy chased her upstairs.

Linny peeked outside later, urine stinging the cuts to her buttocks, but she'd stopped crying. Her attention was drawn to what was missing. She wanted the duck ring, but it was gone. The men must have taken it, the men who took the tiny, dark shape away.

Daddy stayed at work that night. The twins slept in separate bedrooms for the first time in their lives - Linny at one gramma's and Hella at the other gramma's. Mommy and Alexa slept somewhere else.

Tonight, Linny dreams of the duck ring and Daddy and the dark shape under the water, the one who will never cry again and who naps on in the nursery.

*

The twins are beautiful, too: exact replicas of their mother. However, Linny is smarter than her sister. She's learning her letters from television and coloring books. She writes her mother's favorite word in tiny, purple letters inside her drawing tablet: AKWTTD. There are letters missing, Linny knows, and she's frustrated.

Hella grows bored so slides down on the chair until she's almost horizontal and starts kicking the coffee table. Boom ... boom ... boom. Linny shoots her a look that says, *We don't want to take a nap*, and Hella stops.

Mommy's in the kitchen folding sheets. It's Saturday, laundry day. The house smells like the swimming pool: bleachy. Linny hates the smell, so she spends all day trying to breathe through her mouth. She won't go in the swimming pool anymore. The dark shape at the bottom could grab her by the ankle.

AKWTTED, she laboriously prints, tongue lodged in the corner of her mouth. Mommy's word, the one she tells everyone. It's the first word she said to the twins when she saw them again. Hella, who's not as smart as Linny, thought it was Mommy's new name. Linny said nothing, still says nothing.

Maybe it would look better in bright orange crayon.

Crack. She can hear Mommy snap another sheet into a long fold in the air. It's the sound of white. Linny picks up her white crayon instead and prints in big, block letters, AKWITTED. She copies it over and over on sheet after sheet of pulpy white paper until her crayon warps and then breaks in half. To her, it's a sign she's finally got all the letters, so she stops and slows her breathing down until she can inhale through her mouth again. The smell of bleach is making her sick. She doesn't want to throw up on her drawing tablet.

Hella's drowsily sucking her thumb. As if Mommy can see her, her voice singsongs from the kitchen, "Nap-time." Mommy knows best, so the twins stand and climb the stairs, tiptoe past the nursery and crawl into their beds. Linny clutches her drawing pad to her chest. She falls asleep and dreams of a pool chock-a-block with letters, and in the middle, a small, stubby hand rising up from the water, trying to clutch the sky.

*

Morgan smiles to herself and folding the twins' socks. Match, fold, match, fold. When the last sock is paired with its mate, she'll be finished and can go spend some private time with her baby. Brrrr brrrr.

Outside, a breeze creates curls on the pool's surface. It blows past the concrete apron surrounding the water and ruffles leaves of a Jerusalem cherry. Behind the shrub bursting with poisonous, tangerine-colored orbs, pressed against the stockade fence, rests a deflated twist of plastic: a duck ring gritty with one year's raindrops and wind-scattered dirt. A grimy black eye looks up at passing clouds. There's a slash in the eye as if once a child - who was not as intelligent as her twin sister - once took a knife from a kitchen and stabbed the small duck ring to hide it behind the Jerusalem cherry, the only place she could reach before her mommy came back outside, before the men came to take the dark shape away, before they took her mommy away because they couldn't find a child's duck ring in the pool - the one she insisted had been there safely cradling her baby in the water - but not, with any seriousness, believing a woman so beautiful could ever harm her own.

Match, fold. The last pair. Time to get away from the staring gray eyes in the cupboards again.

Mommy's coming, Alexa.

My Night at Rosie's
By William de Rham

After dim sum and a second bottle of hot rice wine, Delancey and I left
The Szechwan Palace to walk up Sansom. A raw March wind whipped
down the dark Philadelphia street no wider than an alley. I'll never
forget how good she felt—her arm clasping mine, her wiry body hard up
against me. I hungered to bury my face in that long, dark mane redolent
of Johnson's Baby Shampoo. My wife Julie and I used Johnson's on our
four-month-old, Trish, so I knew it well.

High heels clicking, Delancey shot me a glance. I was so much taller
than her that she had to look up. Her green cat's eyes sparked in the light
of a street lamp and her mouth, set in marble white skin, was a slash of
rich vermilion. Even now, the thought of that mouth thrills me.

We were going to her place. Sitting side by side in the booth, we'd
agreed. Delancey knew I was married, but she said it didn't matter. She
said all she cared about was how we'd make each other feel; in her living
room, her bedroom, her shower. When, under the tablecloth, she guided
my hand between her legs, that's when I knew she was for real. Julie had
never been so bold, or so exciting.

But first we had to stop at Rosie's. Bobby Boylston, our supervisor at
the district attorney's office, was kicking off his campaign for a seat in
the Pennsylvania State House and Delancey had gotten us invited. It was
my first political bash. I don't know if I was more excited by it, or what
would come later.

Our love of politics was what got me and Delancey together. Both six
months out of law school, and only twenty-six, we were freshly minted
prosecutors, long on theory and short on experience. 'Drooling diaper
babies,' that's what Bobby Boylston called us. Still, with our badges and
our powers to imprison, we thought we were pretty hot stuff and

58

destined for great things. Over brown bag lunches on the great flying stairways of City Hall, we'd talked power and policy, and lusted after the excitement of the campaign trail. We'd even joked about the day they'd give us the White House keys, although we still hadn't decided who would be president and who would be chief-of-staff.

My practical side, forged by my Dad in the cold, dry winters and the hot, parching summers of Montana, told me it was all a pipe dream—especially since Julie hated politics. But the more Delancey extolled my 'charisma' and my 'tall, blond-haired, blue-eyed, Nordic' good looks, the more I thought I just might have a chance.

After all, the hope of a political career was one of the reasons I left Montana for the University of Pennsylvania; that and the basketball scholarship. I figured if Bill Bradley could get to the Senate with an Ivy and the NBA on his résumé, so could I. But a shattered ankle quashed my pro ball dreams and sent me to Penn Law instead. That scholarship was academic.

So I was smart; but not smart enough to keep Julie from getting pregnant or from guilt-tripping me up to the altar. At the time of our wedding, I thought I could make it work. Often my father had said: 'Get yourself a good woman and an honorable trade and the rest will work itself out.' Julie was certainly a good woman: attractive, good-natured, hard-working, and kind. I knew I loved her, especially for giving me Trish, but I didn't think I was in love with her. I certainly didn't burn for her the way I burned for Delancey. And sometimes I resented her for having made me choose a life with her over all the other lives I could have had.

'You're going to love this!' Delancey's silken voice purred as we got to Rosie's. 'It's the place for Republicans to see and be seen.'

It didn't look like much from outside. Just an old, four-story, red brick building layered with a century's worth of soot. It didn't even have one of those big picture windows, like most bars. The windows here were small and covered with grime. Up close you could see they'd been painted black. It seemed pretty shabby.

But all that changed as we stepped inside, our wind-stung faces grateful for the warmth. We stood on a landing overlooking the bar some fifteen feet below. As Delancey handed her full-length fox to the coat-check gal, I stepped to the railing. There was an opulence to the place that reminded me of an 1890s saloon. A crackling fire and a crystal chandelier bathed walls of polished oak in golden incandescence. Red velvet drapes, along with burgundy leather chairs and banquettes, lent a pinkish hue to the brass-railed bar running the length of the room. I expected gilt-framed nudes to line the walls, and was only half disappointed. The frames were gilt, but the paintings were of great stadiums and arenas that had graced Philadelphia through the years: Shibe Park, Franklin Field, the Spectrum, Veteran's Stadium, and others. Once those pictures had been brightly colored, but now, after years of smoke, they were almost sepia. Then there were the photos of the city's great sportsmen—legends like Connie Mack, Lefty Grove, Roy Campanella, Bobby Jones, Bill Tilden, and Reggie White—and all the memorabilia. Rosie's was a monument to Philadelphia sports.

It was busy that night. Every table was full and smoke rose from a hundred cigarettes. Business-suited, the patrons were sleek and prosperous, the most successful of Philadelphians. Yet, despite their success, they wore hungry, dissatisfied looks. I wondered if that was what kept them on top.

Three red-jacketed bartenders worked furiously to serve everyone their drinks while a huge black man with a shiny pate, dazzling white shirt, and emerald tie helped out. When he opened his mouth to laugh, which was often, gold teeth winked. Despite his size, he moved with almost impossible speed. As Delancey tucked her arm in mine and led me down the stairs, I saw him hoist a thirty-gallon tub of ice atop his shoulder and haul it the length of the bar. It must have weighed one hundred pounds, but he handled it as if it were as light as ash. Pouring it into a bin, he shot us a piercing look.

'Isn't this great?' gushed Delancey. 'Look!' she cried, pointing to an old pair of baseball shoes with glistening spikes hanging from a beam. 'Those belonged to Ty Cobb himself. They say he used to sit in the dugout and sharpen them just to intimidate the other team.'

Then she was pulling me through the crowd, up to the bar.

'Rosie! Hi!' she called, waving frantically.

The mountainous man looked over. 'Hey Lancy,' he called back, returning her wave with a pass of his hand as he moved to another customer.

'That's the great Roosevelt Truman himself,' Delancey murmured, her mouth to my ear. Her warm breath was a delight. At that moment, I couldn't have cared less who Rosie was, or about being married, or that we were standing in a room full of people who might someday help get me elected. All I wanted was her.

'He was a Philadelphia Eagle,' she went on. 'One of the last of the NFL's iron men. For twenty years he played defensive tackle and long snap center and never missed a game. Mashed fingers, teeth knocked out, concussions, broken bones—nothing could stop him. And while he was playing, he finished his bachelor's at Temple University and then got his law degree. He's one of the first blacks ever hired by a downtown firm. He's still a partner—still has an office. But he's never there. Says he doesn't need to be to make it rain. He makes plenty of rain right here, and on the golf course. See?'

She pointed above the bar to pictures of Rosie golfing with men like Reagan, the Bushes, Schwarzenegger, Trump, Eastwood, and Nicklaus. Then there were the shots of Rosie with Pennsylvania's power elite: Rosie with its governors, Rosie with its senators, Rosie with Philadelphia's mayors, members of City Council, and even my employer, the fat little man with the million dollar smile who was Philadelphia's district attorney. There were as many Democrats on the wall as there were Republicans. Clearly, Rosie knew how to cross party lines.

'He started out wanting to be a trial lawyer,' Delancey explained. 'Lucky for him his firm made him a deal-maker instead. You want to get anywhere in Philadelphia politics, Rosie's the man to see.'

'How does someone with a name like Roosevelt Truman get to be a Republican?'

'Don't ask. That's why he tells everyone to call him Rosie.'

Just then there was a shrill blast of sound. I looked down the bar to see Rosie holding an air horn. 'OKAY FOLKS!' he bellowed. 'Everyone to the back room to hear our candidate speak. Move along now. Plenty of time for eating and drinking. You want free food and liquor? Got to listen to the man.'

'Rosie!' Delancey called, waving again, as the red-jacketed bartenders herded the crowd. The big man trundled over, his mouth smiling, but his eyes still glaring. 'Rosie, I want you to meet my friend Tom. The one I was telling you about? You take real good care of him, okay?'

'I take care of all my customers, Lancy.'

'I know you do, dear. Tom, be a darling and get me a martini while I go to the powder room. Then we'll hear what Bobby has to say.' Waggling her fingers, she melted into the crowd.

'So, farm boy, what'll you have?' Rosie rumbled as he poured steaming ice into a shaker to make Delancey's martini.

'Wild Turkey.'

'Big drink! Sure you can handle it?'

'Oh, I can handle it.' My face warmed. As he poured gin and vermouth, I grew uncomfortable in the silence.

'How'd you know I grew up on a farm?' I finally laughed in a feeble attempt to charm.

'Hay's still stickin' out your ears.'

Another silence as I struggled for something to say.

'Actually, it's a cattle ranch,' I explained, my cheeks even warmer.

He stirred Delancey's martini.

'But we grow our own alfalfa.'

He poured.

'And grass hay. And oats, for the horses. Not to mention …'

'Boy, I don't care what you and your hick family grow.'

'Hey! We're not hicks!' I cried.

'A hick's a hick,' he insisted, 'and you got hick written all over you. Why don't you stand on top of the bar here and sing us a verse or two of Old MacDonald?'

Now he had me burning. I'd always hated bullies and big-shot or not, this guy was being a bully.

'Hey, jackass!' I shot back. 'Who's doing the serving and who's doing the paying? How about you just pour out the drinks and leave the clowning for comedy night?'

'Boy, do you know who I am?' His head had dropped, and his voice was low, and he reminded me of a bull about to charge. But I didn't care. If my father taught me one thing, it was never to back down from a fight.

'Yeah, I know you. You know me?' I braced myself. 'You think you outweigh me, but I'm taller, younger, and faster, and I haven't been spending my nights in a smoke filled bar. So, what do you want to do? Step outside and get your ass kicked, or serve up the booze and make some dough?'

The man looked me up and down, his fists bunching. I knew what was coming. Back in Montana, I'd been to this point too many times not to. It was another reason I'd left. Too many fights. Now, despite my braggadocio, I was ready for a whupping. Rosie was just too big and strong for it to come out any other way.

But instead of launching himself over the bar, he threw his head back and burst out laughing. 'Delancey sure was right about you! Farmboy hick or not, you really do got a pair!' He stuck out his hand and this time, his smile reached his eyes. 'Put her there kid. I'm Rosie Truman and I'm glad to make your acquaintance.'

For a moment I thought he was faking me out; that he was going to pull me over the bar and stomp me. But his eyes were still kind and I decided to take a chance.

'Tom Swenson,' I said, cautiously taking the hand that was warm, dry, and strong. 'You had me going there,' I admitted sheepishly.

'Little test I used to give to some of the young rooks back in training camp. See what they were made of.'

Before I could ask if I'd passed, a cheer arose from the back room crowd as the candidate took the stage.

'And the drinks are courtesy of Bobby Boylston,' Rosie said, pouring shots for us both. 'Here's to getting to heaven a half hour before the devil knows we're dead, as my Irish friends would say.' With that, we clinked glasses and downed our shots.

'So,' Rosie began, pouring out two more, 'what's a nice married fella' like you doing with a bad ol' gal like Lancy?'

That put me back on my guard. 'How'd you know I was married?'

Rosie glanced down at the ring on my left hand. 'Boy, you want to get anywhere in this town, you *gotta* be quicker than that, and lots less obvious. Now let's try again. What are you doing with Lancy?' Rosie's glare was back.

'Well… we share an interest in politics and Delancey thought I should see what a campaign kickoff's all about.'

Laughter rang from the back room as Bobby got off a joke.

'They certainly seem to like him,' I remarked.

'Any reason they shouldn't?'

'Guess not.'

'But you're not sure?'

I was too young to have learned much discretion. So I just told him.

'I don't care if he is my supervisor, I think he's a horse's hind end. I've never seen anyone carry on the way he does when things go wrong. And nothing's ever his fault. In court last week, Judge Newsome let some kid go on a weapons charge because the lab report said the gun was inoperable. And Bobby, who hadn't even read the report, exploded. I had to drag him out of there before the judge threw him in jail for contempt.'

'Yeah, I heard about that,' Rosie chuckled. 'Well, you're right. Most people do think Bobby's a world class fool.'

'Then how come he's running?'

Rosie looked at me with appraising eyes, as if he were a coach sizing up a new prospect. 'Well now,' he finally began, 'seeing as you and Miss Lancy share an interest in politics, and for the sake of your education, I'll tell you. See the guy standing at the door to the back room? The one with the silver glasses and all that white hair?'

'Yeah.'

'That's Nick Murphy from Lancaster County. He's been a state representative in Harrisburg for the last fifteen years. He's currently the minority leader and if the State House ever goes Republican again, he'll probably be Speaker. He's also a vice-chairman of the Pennsylvania Republican Party, which means he has a say in who runs for what. Now, do you know who the state representative for this district is?'

'Sure, Irv Semple, Appropriations chairman. Everyone knows that,' I said.

'And what party is Mr. Semple with?'

'Democrat.'

'Hear about his DUI?'

'Hear about it? Our office is still getting trashed over that plea bargain. Accelerated Rehabilitative Disposition and community service? I mean, who's kidding who? You're arrested racing down Broad Street on a busy Saturday night, you blow a .17 on the breathalyzer and all you get is ARD?'

'Yeah,' Rosie laughed. 'Well, Irv's afraid come November, the voters'll be thinking the same thing. So, to protect his seat, he made a deal with ol' Nick. There's a new penitentiary about to be built. That means lots of jobs and Nick wants them for his district. And since Irv heads Appropriations, he can make that happen. What's Irv want in return? For Nick to get the Republicans to run a real loser against him—someone who could never win. And that someone, by reason of his shit-bird personality, is your boss Bobby Boylston, who, by the way, is funding his own campaign to the tune of $50,000.00. Signed the second mortgage on his condo yesterday. What do you think about that, farm boy?

'Does Boylston know?'

'Hasn't a clue.'

'Then I think it's pretty corrupt.' I laughed, a little pleased to hear Bobby was getting the shaft.

'I think it's politics,' Rosie replied without a smile. 'And do you know who convinced Bobby to run?'

'Who?'

'Your date. Ms. Delancey Murphy herself. Did it on election night, almost five months ago. Right in the very spot you're standing. Stood there, with her arm through Bobby's and told him how handsome he was and how much charisma he had. Sucker never had a chance.'

'No ... I guess he wouldn't,' I croaked after a moment of silence that felt like forever.

'What'd you say?' asked Rosie, pushing my untouched drink towards me.

'I said why would she do that?'

'Because her Daddy told her to. See, Delancey didn't do all that well in law school and she needed help getting a job. So Papa Nick called me, and I reached across the aisle for Irv and Irv called his fellow Democrat, your boss the DA, and now Delancey has a job.'

'Wait a minute. Nick Murphy is Delancey's father?'

'Boy, where you been? He's a Murphy. She's a Murphy. Didn't I say you better get quick?'

'She never said anything.'

'Yeah, well, she and Nick like people to think she made it all on her own.'

'How come you know all this?'

'Nick and me go way back. Played high school football together when my daddy sent me to live with cousins out near Hershey. He was quarterback. I was his center. He taught me how to spiral the long snap, and that helped get me my start. Then, when I retired from the Eagles, he got me hired by my firm. I was all set to be a public defender. After football, the one thing I always wanted to be was a trial lawyer—get on that big white horse and ride to the rescue. A couple of my professors said I had a real talent for it too, but Nick convinced me I'd do more good if I went with the big boys. Of course, the money helped. NFL didn't pay all that well in those days and being a defender paid even less. Anyway, everything I have—my partnership, my house, this place, all the antiques, plus whatever influence I have—I owe to him.'

'And now that you've helped get Delancey her job and Nick his prison, the debt's paid?' I asked, thinking myself very savvy.

'It doesn't work like that. It's never tit for tat and call it quits. It's about lifelong allegiance—who you've pledged your loyalty to.'

'And God help you if you don't come through?'

'Something like that.'

'Even if it means helping somebody get screwed?'

Now it was me giving Rosie the hard look. But he never flinched. He just stared right back and said, 'Bobby's a big boy. Nobody's holding a gun to his head. He wants to leave the law and come into politics, that's his choice. You want the power and the glory, you gotta pay for it.'

'You make it sound like you regret your choice,'

'I don't regret anything I've done. But sometimes I do wish politics had the clarity of trial work. To me, trials were always a lot like football. You know your objective going in, and who the winners and losers are coming out. In politics, it isn't so clear. Sometimes the right thing gets done for the wrong reason, and sometimes it's vice versa. Lots of times, the things that look right today turn out to be wrong tomorrow and the guy or gal who seems the biggest winner is really the biggest loser. Delancey said you're interested. I just thought you should be clear on what you're getting into. Plus, you're young and I hate to see young talent waste itself.'

'What's that supposed to mean?'

'You know, there's one sure thing about Philadelphia: the longer you stay here, the smaller it gets. Especially for us lawyers. Everybody runs into everybody, sooner or later. I've got this cousin named Effie and she's been Judge Newsome's court reporter for the last fifteen years. Effie knows lawyers the way handicappers know racehorses. And she's been going on and on about this young phenom of an ADA. Tall, blonde guy just out of Penn. Looks like a hick, but can talk the birds out of the trees—at least in a courtroom—according to Effie. A guy who buttered Newsome up so good, he saved Bobby Boylston from going to jail. I've known Newsome a long time. Tough old man. Once his mind's made up, that's it. Anybody who can change it, like you did, has real talent. A talent like that shouldn't be ...'

The rest of his words were lost in a final roar from the backroom. Bobby's talk was over and the crowd was stampeding for the promised food and drink. I turned to see Delancey at the head of the pack, on her father's arm. Rosie came out from behind the bar and embraced his friend. Then he introduced me to the man who could help make my political career.

'Hello young fellow!' Representative Murphy boomed, beaming a winning smile. 'Delancey's told me all about you. Says you're a rising young star.' Sliding his hand over the back of my neck, he came in close. His arm rested heavily across my shoulders. The smoky tang of his Old Spice filled my head. 'Thinks your future might include a move to Harrisburg. Maybe even an extended stay in D.C.,' he whispered, favoring me with a wink.

Then he stepped back, and his voice boomed again. 'You know, we might need someone just like you to run for City Council next year. Now, that's a great place for a young fellow to start! Tremendous arena for getting to know the ways of the world! But you better start saving. Campaigns are expensive! Aren't they Rosie! What did our last run for council cost?'

'About fifty thousand,' Rosie replied softly.

Glancing over, I found him staring into the fire, as if his thoughts were a million miles away. Delancey's hand intertwined itself into mine. It was strong and hard, like the rest of her body and it promised a night of the kind of screaming, sweating, rutting sex that had filled so many of my teenage dreams.

'What do you say we all sit down and discuss it over dinner and a bottle of Rosie's best champagne?' Representative Murphy's smile was bright and his arms were outstretched, as if to gather us in.

Delancey's hand tightened on mine and, all of a sudden, Rosie was back. The expression on his face was searching-like that of an auctioneer about to bring down the hammer for the final time. I'd seen that expression a lot at the government foreclosure sales back in Montana.

I looked at Delancey one more time. She was so beautiful. But for some reason, her touch no longer thrilled. It just hurt. And the mouth I had so longed for—still long for—seemed like a maw. Just then, a whisper of wind tickled my ear, like my daughter's small burp after finishing her bottle. My father's voice rode on that wind: 'Good woman … honorable trade ...' And with it came the knowledge that I was in exactly the wrong place at exactly the wrong time.

I disentangled my hand from Delancey's, and took a step back. 'That's so very kind of you,' I said, 'but really, I can't. It's late and I need to get home to my family.'

Delancey's mouth opened as if she'd been slapped and Representative Murphy's smile froze in place.

'Maybe another time,' I said.

With that, and a wave, I walked back up the stairs and out of Rosie's, leaving Delancey, Nick, and all that might have been behind me.

Day Seven
By Dan Coxon

Day One

She watches him as he drags his suitcase along the hall carpet, leaving dark furrows where the pile has been disturbed. She presses her face closer to the wood of the door, trying to line her eye up perfectly with the crack. She wants to see everything.

This is his third bag so far, and there are boxes piled up in the stairwell too. It looks unlikely that he'll be able to fit it all into the one small bedroom, but she knows spaces can be deceptive. He stops briefly outside her door, wiping his forearm across his brow, the sweat leaving a dark, damp patch on his shirt. She holds her breath until he moves on, then eases herself away from the crack and turns back to her desk.

So far the experiment was going to plan. She'd interviewed five candidates in total, two women and three men. The women were hopeless, far too vapid for her purposes. She figured it'd take an earthquake to get a reaction out of them.

The men were better. The first was Colin, a computer programmer from Essex. He'd moved up here because there were less people, he'd told her. He didn't get on very well with people, you see, and crowds brought him out in a cold sweat. She'd suggested that he was perhaps a bit abnormal, you know, and did he have any mental problems or was he just a weak character? He'd blushed and stammered, stains spreading across the pits of his shirt. Far too reclusive, really. She needed a backbone to break.

Alasdair was different, but no improvement. He was a part-time DJ at one of the local clubs, so any time she wanted tickets, just let him know. Oh yeah, and was it okay if he brought a bird or two back from time to time? Only they wouldn't always let him stay at their place, see. She got rid of him in the end by making unsubtle insinuations that the toilet in the flat upstairs sometimes leaked through the ceiling above the spare bed. She made retching noises behind the door once she'd ushered him out – too much of a sleaze-ball.

Craig had seemed unpromising too, at first. He was a bricklayer, which immediately put her off. He'd be up early each morning, would probably eat out most days, wouldn't bring anyone back. She'd hardly see him, in fact. He just wanted somewhere to crash. It was only once she'd asked him why he was moving out of his current house that she hit gold.

'It's those bloody neighbours, you know? They have these shouting matches in the middle of the night, and I'm not the sort that can get by with only an hour's sleep. So, I figured I'd had enough. I went round there and told them to keep it down. I don't like to get heavy, you see, but they were driving me mad. Anyway, there's been a tension in the air ever since, and I came home the other week to find a turd pushed through my letterbox. I mean, what kind of psycho does that? I figured it was about time to get out of there.'

She smiled. Bingo.

She sits down at the desk and takes out her notebook. She writes 'Day One' at the top of the page. She thinks for a few seconds, and then writes 'Pleasant, friendly, neighbourly' on it.

Then she steps out into the hallway, and asks Craig if he'd like a hand with his bags.

Day Two

She took a while deciding how to play today, but in the end her hand is forced. Craig disappears before she even gets up, a dirty mug left on the worktop where he'd helped himself to a quick coffee before leaving. There's also a note, telling her that he's not likely to be back much before nine. She has all day to think, to plan. She knows she'll only have one chance to do this right.

After her five o'clock lecture she hurries straight home, wanting to be ready for his arrival. She places the dirty mug on the kitchen table, where he can't help but see it, with a bottle of Fairy and some lurid yellow washing up gloves. The message will surely be clear. She also prepares a tape for her nocturnal activities, and sets up the stereo so it faces the wall that separates her bedroom from his. She's already tested it with her knuckles, and was pleased to find that it was little more than plasterboard. The sound should carry well.

By the time he gets home she's almost nodding off, her hectic evening taking its toll. While he slips his boots off in the hallway she drops a couple of caffeine supplements, something to see her through the night ahead. She presses her cheek to the coarse wood of the door again, her eye pressed up to the crack running through it. She can see him loitering in the hall, then walking through into the kitchen. She waits a few seconds, and then the taps start to run. The first bait has been taken.

At ten o'clock Craig turns in for the night, and she eagerly takes the opportunity for a few hours' rest. At midnight her alarm goes off, the volume set down low so that its noise doesn't penetrate the walls. She slips out of bed and tiptoes out into the hall, her socks only making a faint rustling on the carpet, her breathing ragged with excitement in the still night air. Pausing outside his door, she can hear him snoring lightly in his sleep, a sound like the gentle sawing of wood. She tiptoes back to her room, makes a note of the time from her bedside clock, and presses the 'On' and 'Play' buttons of her stereo in quick succession.

Johnny Cash's 'Ring Of Fire' blasts out into the night as she sits at her desk, pen poised above her notebook. She smiles at her own ingenuity, and imagines the grade she'll receive as Craig begins to stir next door.

Day Three

She sleeps in today, to make up for last night. Craig had been polite at first, calmly asking her to turn the volume down a little, but by the third and fourth times of asking she could see him fraying at the edges. She had waited for the soft sounds of his snoring to return once more before turning it back on, this time louder than before. She could almost see him beginning to crack as he came through, the weariness in his voice now replaced with anger. This time she left it off - no use in cracking him too early.

Today marks a change in tactics, a move intended to confuse and disorientate. He'd be feeling that he'd made a mistake by moving in, that last night had defined the way their relationship would stay over the ensuing weeks. He would be wrong. Tonight, he would come home to a different flat.

He's late tonight, a sure sign that yesterday got to him, and she makes a mental note to record this later. When he arrives through the door she comes out to meet him in the hallway.

'Good day on the site?'

He grunts, a non-committal expulsion of air.

'I've made you dinner. To say sorry for last night. Shepherd's pie – I hope you like it?'

'Yes. Thank you. You needn't have – '

'It's okay, it's okay. My treat. You've been working hard, it's the least I can do. Now, do you want it now, or do you want to get changed first?'

He nips into his room to change his shirt, allowing her to light the candles in the kitchen. When he returns the mood is subdued, romantic, another twist designed to confound his expectations. She pulls his seat out for him, giggling girlishly and allowing her breasts to brush against his back. She can almost feel the air of arousal rising off him, his hormones awakened by the contact. Good. All is going according to plan.

They share a bottle of wine over the meal, although she makes sure that he drinks most of the bottle. As she gets ready for bed she leaves the bathroom door slightly open, so that he can see her in her nightdress and underwear as he walks past. She hears him pause briefly by the door as he passes.

She marks it down in the notebook before falling into a deep sleep.

Day Four

Before he returns home tonight she cuts holes in two of his shirts, pulls his belongings from the cabinet drawers and litters them across the floor. She finds some personal letters folded up in the bottom of his sock drawer, so she rips them into little pieces, letting them fall like confetti over the bed. She burns one, just for variety. Then she sits on her bed, and waits.

He's home earlier tonight. Her performance yesterday obviously made him feel welcome. There's a pause as he enters his room, before a cry of 'What the fuck?' can be heard through the wall. Next, the pounding of angry feet, and then a sharp tap on her door.

She waits for a few seconds, preparing mentally for tonight's role, and then shouts out.

'Yeah.'

He crashes through into the room, flinging the door back so hard that it hits the wall. She thinks she sees the crack widen a little. His face shows anger, but also confusion and perhaps, maybe, betrayal. It's details like these that she stores mentally for her notes later.

'Do you know what happened to my room? Someone's trashed it, there stuff everywhere, the whole place has been done over.'

'Yeah, it was me.'

He's baffled, unable to comprehend this sudden switch from flirtation to vandalism over the course of twenty-four hours. She notes that he appears to have a nervous tic in his right hand, a finger that's twitching beyond his control. His left hand clenches and unclenches sporadically.

'You what? Why would you do something like that? I don't understand. Why?'

'As if you don't know.'

A puzzled frown, the cogs of his mind slowly ticking over.

'Did I do something? You can't just go through my stuff, my shirts are wrecked. Are you crazy or something?'

She resists the urge to laugh, to tell him no, it's you that's going crazy. Instead she twists the laugh into a scowl.

'Some girl came round here asking for you today. What's all that about, hey? What about me? I thought we had an agreement, I thought I knew where I stood. Who is she? What are you playing at?'

'A girl?' He starts to grow angry again now, now that he understands. 'Well, I don't know who it was, but why shouldn't she come here? It's not as if you and I – I promised you nothing. I'm sorry if I gave you the wrong impression, but I just want a room here. We're just flatmates. Not lovers.'

She pushes him out into the hallway, managing to shift his weight more through surprise than any great physical feat, and turns the key in the lock that she'd had installed in her bedroom door last week, in preparation.

'I'll see you in hell, you two-timing bastard,' she yells through the door before collapsing onto the bed in a fit of silent giggles. Once the laughter subsides and the air has returned to her lungs she moves across to her desk and records the entire altercation, from start to finish, every detail and nuance that she can remember.

At the bottom of the page she writes – 'Beginning to crack.'

Day Five

Tonight she locks him out of the flat. She knows he'll need to get back in for some clean clothes, so he won't just walk away. She leaves him a sleeping bag and a note out on the stairwell.

When he first gets back he rattles the door in its frame, then she can hear him knocking on all the doors on their floor, asking if anyone knows what's going on. At around midnight he settles down and appears to fall asleep just outside the front door, the sleeping bag wrapped around him. She waits until she can hear him snoring, and then she creeps out and unlocks the door.

She hears him come in at about six the next morning, shower, and then leave again, slamming the door on his way out. She checks that his belongings are still in the room before crawling into bed herself, trying to make up for lost sleep. It's all still there. He's not going anywhere.

Day Six

She has the locks changed while he's out at work, replaced with an identical set that require a new bunch of keys. Just to look at them, you'd never notice the change.

She has to wait by the door this evening, so that when she hears him outside she can open it before he tries his keys.

'You think you can show your face around here still, do you?'

She storms back into the flat before he can reply, trusting his fighting instinct to draw him in. His feet sounding heavy in the hallway as he plods along after her, like a dog on a lead. She notices that he doesn't take his boots off when he enters the house any more.

'What was last night all about? Hey? I slept out on that fucking freezing floor because of you. My back's killing me, I almost fell asleep on the job today. What are these games about? Are you mad, or something?'

She just scowls.

'What? What are you thinking, you crazy bitch?'

'You know what you've done. Don't pretend.'

She turns her back on him, as much to hide the self-satisfied smile on her face as for the effect.

'You're mental. I'm getting my stuff, and moving out of here. One of my mates has said he can put me up for a few days, till I find somewhere else. I'll settle with you later.'

He stomps off to his room and she knows she has to move fast. She runs through to her bedroom, grabs the bag and coat from the bed, presses the play button on the stereo. The CD begins to whirr in its tray as she slams and locks the bedroom door, running up the hallway before Craig realises what's happening. She pulls the front door closed behind her and turns the bright new keys in their locks.

There's no noise as yet. It'll probably take him a few minutes to discover that he's locked in. Maybe a few more to find that the telephone has gone. It'll be at least a few hours before he realises that the CD is looped to play all night. She calls this the Krypton Factor stage, an ingenuity test. A rat in a maze. She can't wait to see how he reacts.

Day Seven

She returns to the flat sporadically throughout the night to check that he hasn't tried climbing out through the windows or sending SOS messages, but from the street the building is silent, dead. She waits until ten o'clock the next morning, two hours after he was supposed to start work, and then she turns her keys in the locks, opening the madhouse for inspection.

It's silent inside, which surprises her. As she walks into the hall she discovers that the door to her bedroom has been burst in, the crack now splitting the entire panel in two. So much for the new lock. There are scratches and dents along the walls as she walks towards the living room, as if someone has been punching and tearing at them with their nails. She thinks she sees specks of blood in one of the dents, although she can't be sure.

Her mouth is open as she rounds the corner into the living room, expecting the worst, but the room is relatively intact. A few cushions have been thrown on the floor, but nothing is broken.

It's as she takes a step inside that she feels the heat of his breath behind her, and she turns and staggers backwards into the room. There's not much time to make many mental notes as he rushes at her, although she does notice that his eyes look like they're popping out of his skull, his knuckles bloody and beginning to scab over as he lifts the crude club above his head, a piece of skirting board pulled away from the walls, the nails still sticking through the splinters.

He says nothing, only grunts as he swings it down for the first time.

Barney Jones
By Samantha Priestley

A few days ago it all started up again. That feeling. That same feeling Kelly had all those years ago with Barney, and it scared her this time.

Mark parroted something off about hormones rushing in Kelly's body: weird ones, he said, that she didn't even know were there. What were these things then? She tried to imagine them. Electricity. Sparks. No, that wasn't right. Mark probably had the scientific explanation. He could probably give it to her in terms of circuit boards and impulses. Impulses. That was more like it.

She opened her eyes to the click of the central heating, filling the house with warmth. Running hot water. Radiators drying straggly wet clothes. Mark got up, his bulk leaving a sag in the mattress. Kelly hated the mornings now. They felt forced. She hated the things she had to do. Making breakfast. Straightening beds. Cleaning teeth and brushing hair. Not what a morning should be.

She pulled the covers back around her throat, wanting to go back to the dream she kept having. The one about a war. The one with stealth bombers and the screams of ill-informed men. Shouting and lunging like drunks on a Saturday night. Beautiful men.

It was a long time since Barney had left but Kelly thought she still knew where he was. She watched people like him on the news, smiling on the backs of trucks, legs and arms spilling out like beans. Uncontrollable. She saw their dirty faces, their bulky uniforms. The enemy were soft sheets. Perfect skin and sleepy eyes. The khaki lay in folds about their bodies, white cloth billowing in the wind, flapping around their ears. They adored their weapons. They held them like babies. Kelly tipped her head and gazed into their eyes on the TV screen hoisted high in the corner of the bedroom. No one loves fear that much. Nobody wants to die. Not until they're left with nothing.

She got up, washed her face and took the weight of a bathrobe on her shoulders and back. Mark was already downstairs. Kelly could hear him, boiling the kettle for her cup of tea. He was so good at taking care of her, she thought. Maybe too good, she could hardly do without him.

She felt her legs heavy on the stairs as she went down, already dreading the day. In the kitchen Mark was eating toast, the hot mug of tea waiting by the kettle.

Kelly dipped behind him and slipped his car keys under a mat on the table while he wasn't looking.

'I don't know what we're going to do about this one,' he said, guiding an electric razor over his face while he held the half eaten toast in his other hand and glanced up at the TV. He shook his head a little. 'I mean, how do you fight an enemy like that? We don't even know where they are.'

Kelly wondered who 'we' were. Would 'we' be doing the fighting?

'I wish you weren't going,' she said. It stuck her for a moment how painful her voice sounded, how pathetic. As if Mark was going to war.

Mark stopped shaving. 'What do you mean?' he asked.

'Don't go in today. You know I need your help with the kids. I can't do it on my own.'

'Don't start, Kelly.' He put his jacket on and shoved his hands in his pockets. 'Have you seen my keys?' he asked.

She shook her head.

'Oh not again. What have you done with my car keys? I have to get to work Kelly.'

His anger showed at the edges. It was never full blown. It snagged and pulled like cotton.

She shook her head again.

Mark began pushing things around on the kitchen worktops. Breakfast plates and a sludgy coffee cup he'd already drunk from. Marmalade smeared knife and greasy place mats. He moved over to the table and did the same. The keys tinkled and betrayed Kelly. Mark grabbed them and went striding through the door, shouting over his shoulder, 'You'd soon complain if I didn't have a job, wouldn't you? Be different then.'

A baby is asleep upstairs just able to touch the sides of his carrycot if he stretches out his arms. Blue and green checks, soft and padded. Tactile fabrics and a terry toweling sheet covering the plastic mattress. He lies on his back, one blushed cheek turned to the warmth of his bed, his arms above his head in complete security. All babies look like this. It's uniform. Their little hands only just unraveled like a tapped chocolate orange at Christmas.

Downstairs a two-year-old girl cranes her neck to see the TV, her crossed legs rammed right up against the cabinet, her nose almost touching the screen.

This one is still pretty, thinks Kelly. Still a little elf whose eyes flicker across the TV, fingers and toes, knees and elbows fidgeting.

Nevertheless, Kelly knows she had children too early. She was eager to give everything up for the little wrinkled noses and downy heads. Ready to say goodbye to her fast life and become a mother. She is aware of all that. They were like locks and keys. Putty dreams. Meant to secure her future. They were supposed to detract from all her mistakes.

The lunchtime news is much worse than this morning's. Hysterical. People running in the streets of a faraway country. Children. Women. Old men. And somewhere in all of this, Kelly thinks, is a man she once loved. A man she hasn't seen for years. How many years? She tries to count them.

It was the summer at the end of their last term in school when life still seemed like it was all worth playing for. They spent their last year goofing around, Kelly and Barney. Sneaking about down hidden sides of the building. Slipping through swinging doors. Into toilet cubicles to smoke and do God knows what else. Ducking out on Friday afternoons. Can you be in love at fifteen? Kelly was always the level-headed one. Yeah, she got drunk like everyone else and she fooled around with Barney, but how could she have known what love was back then?

It's hard to remember now, who ran away first. Him to the army or her to another city, a new beginning. Away from his 'we're meant to be' stuff. Away from her mum's disapproval and the family arguments. She guessed it was her. Cutting loose and not caring if she never saw the lot of them again.

The baby is crying. A perfectly spaced sound. Kelly puts her hands over her ears for a moment and paces the hall, breathing slowly and deeply as if she can stop the pain. She never imagined she could feel so lost here, with all she's ever wanted around her. Why is it so difficult just to live and be happy? She could run away again, like she did the last time it all got too much. She could break from the house now and leave with only her old jeans and a T-shirt. But at twenty-one it seems too much like a habit to do it again. And she has babies now. And a husband.

*

Mark tries to phone her mid-morning. He hesitates with his fingers over the buttons. She might beg him to come back, give him some story about the baby being ill or how she thinks she'll go mad on her own there. He weighs the receiver in his hand. Last week he drove home in the afternoon when she'd rung up crying, sobbing down the line and babbling incoherently about how low she felt. But this week seemed so much worse. It's a woman's thing. He supposes he'll never fully understand this. Hormones. Postnatal. Depression even? He's tried to make her see that she's only going through the same thing thousands of other women do. It's about having babies, isn't it? The way nature takes over and kicks in.

He dials the number and waits for her voice. He doodles on the pad of paper on his desk. Rockets. Bullets. He remembers something and writes the word 'christening'. Have they arranged everything for the baby's christening? He'll ask her now when she answers. He butts the pen on the pad. There's no answer.

Kelly has been at the hospital for nearly an hour. Her baby has stopped crying now. A paediatrician expertly fastens the poppers on the baby's little sleep suit, covering his round tummy, spongy like the give in an inflatable.

'He's fine.' the paediatrician says.

There was an infection in what would become a tummy button. Hard and scabby where a midwife had severed mother and son. It still poked out. An obscene little jut on his middle. The doctor tells Kelly she should wash it carefully every day with cold boiled water. 'Twice a day,' he adds. Then he looks at her as if he doubts her capability. 'Any more problems, bring him straight back,' he says.

Kelly smiles at the doctor. She must look like one of those poor exhausted mothers who live below their own expectations. She wants to tell him she was a competent woman. Intelligent. Funny in her day. Never short of company. But somehow she can't stand the sound of it in her own head.

The next morning the heating clicks on the timer. The baby is already awake today, bawling for the breast. Mark slides from the bed and dresses quickly. Kelly pushes the button on the TV and hears the car's engine wheeze outside. The colour from the screen shines on her skin. Bloodless. She runs out of the house after Mark and stands in front of the car, her upper body pushed onto the bonnet.

The troops have gone in. It was on the news. Brown bodies running. Khaki jackets billowing. It's being blown to pieces, half of the world.

Mark thumps the horn inside the car. 'Kelly!' he shouts. 'Get out of the way.'

She stretches her arms over the car, fingertips almost touching the bottom of the windscreen. Like a martyr. She scrutinises the paintwork beneath her. What is her cause? The deep brown eyes of men about to kill someone she once knew? Murder in the East? Or is it about herself again?

Mark is winding the window down and pushing his head out. Undoing his seatbelt and standing in his seat. 'Kelly,' he says. 'What's going on? What's the matter?'

'I can't do it,' she mutters. 'I can't cope. I can't stand being on my own here.'

*

82

The crouching man could never have been seen. One knee touched the ground, the other supported him. He fired something that looked like a kind of ancient musical instrument. The kickback shook his body as the grenade left its launcher, but he was already getting used to it.

Kelly dreamt that Barney was blown to pieces by a man like this. Shrapnel tore open his body. She wondered for hours after, would he have suffered? Or would he have been fortunate enough to be caught directly by the blast?

Soldiers must live their lives from minute to minute. How do they do it? They must eat and sleep out there with the clawing worry of death.

Mark shifts beside her in the bed again, one arm folding over her hand. It's nighttime now, but he's awake.

'Why didn't you phone me yesterday? I would have taken you to the hospital,' he says.

'It doesn't matter. Anyway he's fine.'

'Yeah. Don't tell your mother though. She's bound to say it was my fault.'

For a moment there is a blissful well of happiness and Kelly slowly dips her toes. She peels away years and feels, after all, how she always felt about Mark.

'Don't be stupid' she says. 'Mum adores you. You're the one thing I've done right.'

She listens for the baby, but he must be asleep. She still gets that awful panic when she can't hear him.

'I've taken the whole week off work so you don't need to worry,' Mark says. Kelly sits herself up on her elbow in bed. What does he think she should be worried about? Her mother? The stress of the christening? Or has she persuaded him, with all her outrageous behaviour, of the one thing she's always been afraid of? That Kelly is a bad mother. That she can't do it. That she is useless, hopeless, and she needs Mark there just to be on the safe side.

Mark turns the wheel in his hands. Leather pulled tight. The baby has slept all the way to Kelly's mum and dad's house and the little girl sings and scribbles on books. Mark's suit is hanging by one of the back windows. The baby tries to focus on the shape. Staring. His beautiful eyes working. Mark squeezes Kelly's knee as they turn into the drive. She has to admit he's trying. He had this romantic idea that they could do this whole christening thing in the church they were married in. It was only a fluke they were married there anyway. Only because Kelly's mum got wind of Mark's clumsy proposal and would hear of nothing but a big wedding in the family church. It makes Kelly think of the lines of tombstones out in the graveyard with her ancestors' names chiselled into the stone, and how she'll probably be expected to follow them all into one of those as well.

They drag their bags to the door. Kelly's mum flings it open and feigns a kiss on each of her daughter's cheeks. Kelly has a sudden panic. Mark better not be planning to stay here all week.

Kelly carries her baby in a ridiculous long gown thing. Something else her mum insisted on. Kelly can't stand all this ritual paraphernalia. It stifles her. Mark holds his candle and mutters his words. 'I promise to renounce the devil.'

Kelly wants to laugh. The devil isn't here. Not with them today.

Mark winks as they sit back down. Of course he doesn't believe in such things as heaven and hell. Men don't, do they?

Kelly's dad sits in his old armchair after the christening, lifting a finger to the TV and prophesising about what he sees.

'RPG.' he says. 'Rocket propelled grenade. Mass produced they are.' He turns back to his oldest friend who sits watching the news bulletin with him.

'Russians use them as currency, don't they? And that place is saturated with them.'

They nod together, stuck in some kind of mutual backwater, distancing themselves from war.

Kelly watches.

Why do people get pulled with tides?

Mr. Jones is Barney's father. Kelly's old lover wrapped in loose skin. The same eyes. Crooked walk. The same life-weary voice. Kelly thinks he could never have loved like his son did. She can see no spark of passion in this man. But far from thinking his son would grow into him, she wonders how the same DNA can possibly be twisting inside them. He was such a live wire, Barney, always good for a laugh. Kelly just didn't want to go out with a joker anymore. That was the top and bottom of it. When they left school she said he should grow up, get a job, start getting serious. Only not with her.

She watches her mum touch her dad's shoulder and she sees the way he reacts. Instant, like a reflex. Kelly's dad leaves his friend floundering in mid-sentence to give his wife his attention. It's undivided. Surely they can't still have love between them? Not after all these years. Surely Kelly and Mark will never grow into this kind of comfort. They will keep their individuality, their own space. Isn't it true that every generation is younger for longer? Kelly glances at the fuzzy photograph of her grandmother on the mantle. Browning round the edges. She must only have been about fifty there, yet Kelly can never remember her looking any different to that. Old before her time. Following her peers into the same print dresses, court shoes, tan tights and corsets. We don't do that anymore, do we? We are singular. We have our own minds. We care less what others think of us.

'Have you heard from Barney, Mr. Jones?' Kelly asks.

She is taking one step out into the terrifying silence. Aware that nobody speaks about this.

'Of course dear.' Mr. Jones says.

Kelly's mum shoots her a glance. She always expected too much, her mum. She always had this idea that Kelly could do better. She pushes past Kelly and mutters, 'Don't ask questions like that, it's rude. You can see he's worried. Besides, we don't need reminding about you and Barney Jones.'

Of course. No one wants to be reminded of that. Mark is glaring at Kelly now. Yeah, they all know about her and Barney Jones. They all know it was her fault he went to war.

Kelly glances at the photo of her grandmother again. Frozen in one of those promenade pictures. Walking, her arm thrust around her sister's. Crowds of people broken into without them knowing. If only Kelly could do that. Stop it all. Stop time. No one would be any the wiser. If only she could go back and persuade Barney to take a job in a bank or get into computers or something. Why did he always have to be so reckless? She'd tell him she didn't care. It wouldn't matter to her what he did. It would never be enough anyway. She just doesn't want to feel guilty about him all her life. His family had even stopped speaking to hers for a while after Barney went away. And there's his dad, supposed to be best mates with Kelly's dad. She did that. Split everybody in half. She heard they almost came to blows over it.

Kelly goes over and sits on Mark's knee, dragged down by guilt and 'what ifs'. Families are so complicated. All that tip-toeing about. Not ruffling feathers. Why do we bother? She's chosen her partner, why does she have to bother with family politics?

They turn the TV off. Kelly's mum appears with a tray full of champagne glasses filled with fizzy wine. They want a toast. Something to set the moment apart.

Kelly and Mark's daughter runs through from the kitchen with a boy in pursuit. Her bobbed hair flapping. A shriek. A giggle.

'This is what it's about,' Kelly's dad says. He holds his glass in the air and gestures to the baby tucked away in his car seat, dozing in a corner. There are bubbles of 'yeah', 'that's right' and 'certainly is' coming from the other guests. Kelly shifts on Mark's knee, looking at her baby son. Things will be different for him. She'll make sure of it. He has it all in front of him. But Kelly can't help feeling sad at the thought. She grasps the stem of her wine glass. Can she really expect to change the world for him? Maybe Barney is out there doing that. Maybe she should be glad she pushed him to go, even if her family will always have that look when his name comes up. Nearly tore us apart that business.

She feels for Mark's hand. What did he say? Hormones. Impulses. He told Kelly that having babies is a funny kind of nature. Does all sorts of things to a woman. And what about a man? What does it do to them?

She notices her dad looks like he's close to tears. She doesn't think she's ever seen that before.

'This little boy sleeping here, not even knowing what's going on,' he says. 'He's what it's all about.'

And Barney's dad leans over, glances up at Kelly, filled with an unknown war his son has gone off to fight. It's all right, his look seems to say to Kelly, I understand. He understands why she did it, why it could never work. He understands why Barney had to go, and he isn't blaming anybody anymore. Things just happen and they all, including Kelly, have to look forward. They'll go mad if they don't.

'Yes,' Barney's dad agrees. 'The next generation. That's what it's all about.'

Burden
By Shannon Bates

As you rotate the jewel case of the CD, gingerly turning the corners of the plastic box with your broad fingers, you curse the fat that has invaded your hands. It ballooned from your ass, through your thighs, over your knees and around your ankles. It inflated from your belly, to your nearly feminine breasts, out through your elbows and encircled your wrists. You had been fighting it for years, passing as a chubby or stocky boy, but by eighteen years old, it has caught up with you beyond your worst nightmares. You must now wear suspenders to help support your enormous pants. You can no longer see your own shoes as you transport your cumbersome body weight from place to place.

'Excuse me,' a bold voice interjects from behind you. You squeeze as well as you can to become flat against the rows of compact discs, hoping that the aisle is wide enough for this lanky man to slip by. The wooden shelf sighs with the weight of your hips against it. You feel the brush of a thick chain, which swings from the other man's belt loop toward his knees and back up to disappear into his pocket. These walkways are far too narrow for any comfortable passing, but you feel that the fault is yours.

'Sorry,' you mumble, as the man negotiates his way past. His jet-black hair and sideburns, inky surf sweatshirt and oversized, charcoal cargo pants whisk away. You watch as this lean body escapes you—a slim shadow unhinging itself from your person.

You replace the CD you were studying, flipping through the G's to insert it in the appropriate alphabetical order. You decide that the used cassette tapes in the bin on the open floor will better suit your needs and you exit the cramped aisle.

It is here that you first see her as she drifts in through the glass door. She takes your breath away; just as she did the first time you met her. Her beauty is no longer that of a child, but of a woman, though she has barely passed fifteen years old. Her cheeks do not merely glow, but are radiant. Her eyes blaze far beyond the crisp sparkle that once danced there. Her hips are alive, even as she remains still, filling the entranceway with her provocative presence. Her neck arches gracefully with the wisdom no child dares learn. The platinum strands of her soft hair now flow uninhibited down her narrow back.

You want her, but not as you did before. Not to break her, but to love her.

You watch her as she scans the store with determination, her mouth pouting thoughtfully. Her beauty has not escaped the sight of every other man in the room, either. Their eyes dart sideways as they pass her, instinctively lowering their aim to observe the full package. Her slim, black top and denim shorts invite their eyes to wander. They peer longingly at her collarbone, her ankles, her waist; just as they would study any other beautiful woman. But she is not a woman. Despite her allure, she is still only a girl, as she was when you met her two years ago.

She glances in your direction, then she turns and begins to wander down the furthest aisle from you. It is the Country and Western section, which she hates. You remember this bit of trivia with a fondness that suggests that you knew her more intimately than anyone else did. You did, in a way, but not the way that she had wanted. She was so naïve, so innocent. She had even been gracious when she finally told you six months later to stay away from her. She was apologizing, telling you that she didn't want you to call her anymore. It was at this point that you began to lose control of your weight, inch by inch, pound by pound. The fat obscured your view of what you had done, coating your filthy hands with deceptive softness. It tucked away that person deep inside its layers.

She must have seen you here in Tower Records, standing in the uncluttered main floor area. She has moved from your view, but still you gaze dreamily at the doorway from which she entered. Your plump hands rest on a Whitesnake cassette with a cracked case. Looking down suddenly, you yank your fingers from the discount bin. Of course she saw you. Your waist is broader than the listening booth. Your body is rounder than the giant, dangling promotional CD cutouts above your head. Perhaps she didn't recognize you. You sigh and lumber dejectedly toward the door.

As you approach the jazz section, she reappears suddenly, stepping across the checkerboard tiles toward the cashier. Her lean legs move swiftly as you harness the momentum of your huge thighs to keep from colliding with her.

'Hey, Kitten!' you blurt, before you can prepare yourself with a follow-up conversation. You call her by the nickname that you gave her, hoping that she will gush at this opportunity for nostalgia.

She does not.

There is a stutter in her stride, and she takes a step backward. In her stunning face, you see fear disguised by practiced confidence. It is an unsettling expression. Her eyes are so green. You notice that the fire here is not passionate, but an eerie, simmering blaze. Her mouth is so full and strong. Can she no longer smile? You want to touch her. You want to discover that her skin is still as silky as it was. This unfamiliar power she now has seems to steal all of your composure, and to drain all of your determination.

You clear your throat, and she finds her voice.

'Hey…' The sharp tail of this word drags beneath her teeth in a sour, gravelly vowel. This makes you nervous, and so you laugh lightly, almost as if you are stifling a cough.

'How have you been?' you ask. You are sincere. You want to know. It has been a long time since you have seen her—her radiant skin, her angular jaw, the sexy curve of her lower back. You have wanted to know how she is doing every day of every month. You have driven by her house, slowing a little as you passed, just to be near her. You have asked all of her friends about her, but they offer no details of interest. You have stared at the phone, trying in vain to create a reason to call. And here she is, alive and gorgeous, standing in front of you.

'I've been okay,' she lies, and you want to believe it. You want to believe that you caused no pain, but you know better. It's almost empowering to know that you affected her life so deeply. She even stopped spending her lunch hours in the open air of the campus quad.

She completely disappeared from the sunlight and from the main walkways of the high school. Her shimmering presence no longer fluttered about the edges of your life. You lost her in the shadows and the corners. If only it hadn't been so negatively that you affected her life, then maybe you could somehow still be proud to have known her. But here, as you watch the empty burning of her beautiful eyes, you don't feel anything like pride, deep in your well-insulated gut.

You cock your head at her, asking silently for details.

'Lots of stuff is going on,' she offers. She shifts her weight and pivots her right knee in and out, with her shoe poised upon its toe. She fidgets with the CD she has chosen to purchase. You see the cover of the Charlie Parker album and smile. You had held many discussions about the late saxophone player's genius.

'Yeah, me too.' You also lie, but with a smile. You want her to believe that you've been content, but you know that she is not fooled. 'Uh, would you like to get together sometime?' Your face does not burn with a reflection of your anxiety, but your stomach turns as you try to read her expression. Her eyes stare back at you blankly. They are not blank with ignorance. They do not betray her intelligence. Rather, there is a blankness in her expression that brews with calculating precision. Her eyes are an intense green, slightly narrowed, as if to discipline you – as if to persuade you to think your words over once more and come up with an answer on your own.

You don't speak.

'No,' she responds at last, with no emotion in her voice. You are the one to take a step back this time, startled by this woman's voice. The girl you met two years ago didn't have such a voice, so resonant and assertive.

With an enticing stretch of her arm, she sets down the CD that she has been holding, and it comes to rest with a tidy snap against a display of blank tapes. The cover photo of Charlie Parker's face glows under the wash of fluorescent lights. She turns her shapely shoulder and strides confidently away from you.

Her answer stumps you. In your most insecure thoughts, you never saw it coming. You hadn't counted on such a sure rejection. She had always left a courteous window open for you, but not now. Yet, in all fairness, you cannot claim that this is the first time that she has said no to you.

You can recall now the moment when her hips were set ablaze, reluctantly in your hands. Your fingers were slender then—eager and agile against her pristine skin. Her body twisted and squirmed to keep the door shut. *Not you*, it said. *Not now*. But you pressed on. Her voice said the same – that sweet, polite, deep voice. *No. Please, no*. You had argued that she was too tempting. You craved more than just a kiss, more than just her arms around you. You needed her flesh against yours, even as she shivered. You had to get inside her somehow. You couldn't let her go, no matter how she begged to escape. It just wouldn't be fair if you weren't allowed to have her.

But you didn't ever really have her. You took her away. You stole her. But you couldn't keep her. She slipped through your fingers as you tightened your grip on her flesh. You stared her down hungrily as the flame lost its passion. The sweetness of her skin burst and spilled out onto the sheets, leaking from her pores in an unsalvageable flood. This had at once made you feel so dominant, so invincible.

You watch her now as she walks away, never looking back. Her body is sleek and taut, like a cat that is no longer a kitten. You watch her hips sway in a compact figure eight, and her calves tighten and relax above her thick-soled tennis shoes. She has grown up, perhaps too quickly, and she must now carry herself as a woman.

You stand with your feet far apart to sustain your sprawling girth. You are heavy with guilt. Heavy with the burden of having stolen a girl's innocence, her mystery, her serenity, her spark. This is weight that you will never lose.

The Baby in the Cupboard
By Paolo A. Gardinali

She had to lean back against the white rental Chevy. It's the heat, she thought. Her eyes closed as she fanned herself with the Orlando street map she had picked up at the airport's Avis. There had been snow in Mexico, NY, lots of it. Two feet overnight, and she'd almost postponed the trip again. It had just seemed too obvious an excuse. She took slow breaths until her sense of balance was restored. Carefully folding the map, and putting it away in her purse, Maria straightened her glasses and looked at the place. Picture perfect palm trees framed the entrance-way to the self-storage facility. The building was brown stucco with red tiles and didn't look as bad as she'd expected. But she still felt out of place, her midseason green blazer inadequate, her underthings already made uncomfortably wet by perspiration.

Why people came here for vacation, she could not comprehend. Why people would live or choose to die here, she could not fathom. She was surrounded by shiny islands of concrete and glass wrapped in ribbons of asphalt, anonymous sedans with darkened windows, and older men sipping martinis early in the day, wearing garish shirts, in exotic-themed hangouts. She had not felt like eating much, and had just sat in her booth with a shrimp salad with too much mayo, hiding behind a paperback. It was not unusual for her to have stacks of books protecting her from the outside world, providing sanctuary, employment, or simply diversion. In the diner she had found herself procrastinating again, picking at the salad, people-watching, and postponing the inevitable.

Once more she made herself get up and move, walking towards the building.

'My name is Maria, Maria Maggione.' She handed an open envelope to the man behind the counter.

'You guys sent me this bill. I'm here for my parents'… stuff.'

Packing materials filled the small office. Sample cardboard boxes, dangling from the ceiling, rotated and were slowly propelled by ceiling fan currents, their price marked in red sharpie on each side. The attendant looked at her blankly, an unlit cigarette hanging from his lower lip. He looked at the letter and then scanned an antediluvian Rolodex, pulling out an index card and two small brass keys taped over a large UNPAID stamp mark. The man did not say a word, just pushed the keys across the counter towards her and pointed outside to the left, never once looking her in the eyes.

She followed the numbers to the storage space 313, walking down the unending corridor, one red door after the other, her faint shadow dancing on the walls, projected by the fluorescent lights. Her red door was no different from the others. The key worked fine, the hinges did not creak. Inside, the smell was of old things; a faint aroma of dust, motor oil and ageing upholstery. She fumbled for a switch, and the bare light bulb wired to the ceiling blinded her for a few seconds. The space inside was cramped, the ten by fifteen unit crammed with furniture and boxes. Her fingers traced parallel tracks in the dust over the familiar faux oak TV cabinet. She looked at the green velour couch and remembered all the imaginary enemies she had fought back from the forts built with its heavy pillows.

She stood there for a few seconds, that familiar feeling of light-headedness surrounding this compressed version of her childhood. The light was weak and yellow, and she cursed herself for not even bringing a flashlight. She opened an old cabinet. It was stuffed with what could have been old tablecloths, or perhaps pillowcases. She peeled back the newspapers, unwrapping their contents: old china. She pulled out a large piece of cloth, carefully laid it on the closest corner of the couch, and sat down on it. She took off her glasses, blew away the dust gently from the lenses, and then wiped them carefully with a Kleenex. Nothing had any value, really, just worthless forgotten pieces from a previous life. There was nothing she could sell to pay the outstanding storage bill. If she was really lucky she might find some goodwill store willing to haul out the whole load for free.

She pulled the TV cabinet's door open. The TV was gone, replaced with stacks and stacks of papers. She should check that nothing too personal was left, but some faded pictures and financial records of long-extinguished accounts could not matter that much. She pulled out a bundle of letters, tied by a dark green ribbon, flipping through them like they were playing cards, and recognized her mother's delicate handwriting. She dropped the letters in her purse. She would need to buy some of those overpriced cardboard boxes and pack up all the papers to sort through later, just in case. The rest could go; she had no space left in her life.

Her eyes focused on the dark shape in the corner of the storage unit. It looked like an old armoire. She had never seen it in her parents' condo, and could not place it at the old Jersey house. The piece was made of dark wood, walnut perhaps, and it had the slightly irregular charm of the hand crafted. She tried to move around the stack of chairs to get to the armoire, resolving to move them out in the corridor, one by one. Inserting herself in the space she had just freed, Maria pushed her back against the wall and moved the TV cabinet just enough to face the armoire. She pulled on the wooden knob. It resisted for a while, the large, thick door deformed by humidity. It finally opened with a pop - freeing the sweet smell of time and uncured wood. It was almost empty, except for some crumpled newspapers pushed all the way against the far wall. When she tried to pick up the newspaper, something heavy rolled out of it. An old doll, with a large head and the tiniest limbs. One of her old toys, maybe? Pulling away the crumbling newspapers she saw the doll's face, but it had the features of a decrepit little man, the skin was taut and almost nonexistent yellow lips pulled over a toothless, unnatural grin.

She remembered falling. Hard. She remembered her chin hitting the bare wooden planks of the floor of the storage unit and bumping her head against the coffee table, scratching her hands and knees as she tried to scramble out on four legs, like a dog. Grabbing an old chair to pull herself up, she bent down again to vomit the rest of the salad onto the dusty corridor floor. The cigarette man looked at her when she rushed back into the office.

'There's a baby,' she said. 'There's a baby in the cupboard.'

Later, she was sitting in the back of a squad car, wrapped in a brown ordinance blanket, sipping lukewarm coffee with too much non-dairy creamer and sugar. In her left hand she still held a piece of the old newspaper.

Men in uniform were walking around. Yellow tape. Some guy barked orders while talking on a cellphone. She saw the attendant finally talking, or rather, waving his arms in front of an officer, in some parody of an animated conversation. She was too far away to hear.

Her stomach felt queasy, she tried not to think about it, about those dark holes where the baby's eyes had been, about the bundle of dry flesh she had held for an instant. Shrunk like a *tsanta*. She wondered about a drink of water, they had offered her a glass when they brought her to the station. She had declined. She was afraid to ingest any more liquids, afraid that she might need to use the bathroom; afraid she would have to ask.

She was sitting on the wooden bench with all those people. What had they done? What had she done? They all seemed to know better, aware of what they had to do and what they had to say. It was like when she was in school and was never sure of herself. She recalled playing with her many cousins, who made fun of her. They were darker, miniature versions of their moms and dads. She had felt awkward with her pale skin, her almost reddish hair, sitting alone in the corner of the garden, on a bench, like now, singing to herself or telling a story to her imaginary brother.

A squat mustachioed man was talking on the phone, his head reclined on one side of the receiver, his uniform collar undone. He gestured at people on the bench as he spoke, singling out someone to stand, and they stood up hesitatingly, holding a piece of paper or holding nothing at all. She closed her eyes.

Santina approached her bed, a dark, thin shape in the shadows of her small bedroom. Daylight was barely filtering through the lowered shades, just enough to redraw the sharp edges of her mother's figure in blinding white contours.

'How are you feeling, Maria?'

'My throat hurts, Mama.'

'Santa Madre, you still running a fever.'

Maria felt Santina's cool hand on her forehead. It was a small hand, a hand already old, a hand that was old even before she was born. Wiry, calloused fingers that felt like they had dug their way across continents.

'I'll send your father down to the store to get you *il gelato*.'

'Can I have gelato for dinner?'

'Now, we don't want to make a habit of this, just for tonight, *vabbene?*" smiled Santina.

Maria closed her eyes again. She imagined her father, down in the sitting room on the recliner, smoking in front of the TV. Her father looking her way and not seeing her, tired after his unending day of work. She never thought for a moment he would actually go down to the store, or simply smile to her, worry about her temperature.

'Do you want me to tell you a story?'

Maria nodded weakly. She closed her eyes, pulled the blankets up to meet her chin, and waited.

'Once upon a time, on an island far, far away, lived a King and a Queen. The King and Queen had lands that extended to the horizons, and coffers full of coins of Roman gold and jewels. Their halls were lined with Greek statues and their cellars held barrel after barrel of the sweetest *Malvasia* wine. The peasants loved them: they brought them fat young piglets to roast, and the most beautiful white stallions to ride. But the King and Queen were very unhappy. In the big stone castle, overlooking the sunny hills, no sound of little feet echoed, no cry and no shrill laughter were ever heard. Days passed, the King wisely governing the land, and the Queen gathering the women to teach them the art of the loom and the Gospel of Our Lord. But no babies were born. One day, an old lady no one had seen before was weaving alongside the others. The Queen stopped by to check on her work, and did not recognize the lady, who appeared more ancient than the olive trees that lined the hill. The cloth that she was weaving was pale pink and so marvelously soft, like the skin of a newborn baby. The Queen frowned.

"What is your name?" The Queen asked.

"I am Nona," the old lady replied, "and if I may dare to speak frankly to Your Majesty, the thing that She most desires is there within the grasp of a faithful woman."

"What do you mean?" asked the Queen.

"Your Majesty, even the greatest rulers of this earth have to kneel in front of a higher authority. If Your Majesty were to do so, and made sure she did not forget Nona, all her wishes would come true."

The Queen was upset at the tone of the old woman, but what she had said touched her. She dismissed the women, and retired to her quarters. The Queen spent the next nine days praying. She did the Novena on her knees, refusing anything to eat or drink, dedicating her suffering to Saint Agatha. On the tenth day, the King visited her, and touched her feverish head with his large, cool hands. And when he left the room, the Queen was with child.

A church was built to Saint Agatha, and across the countryside the people waited with bated breath for the royal birth. When the baby was born it was a beautiful boy with curly blond hair, and the Queen held it up to the crowd gathered under the castle's windows, and a night of celebration was declared. Many were invited to pay homage to the crown prince, but the mysterious old Nona was left out.

"Perhaps she is dead by now," thought the Queen, "and in any case, I shall not have to see that wizened old lady on such merry a day."

In the morning, the Queen was awakened by a blood-curdling scream. Rushing to the baby's cradle, she almost collided head-on with the screaming servant.

"What is it?" The Queen asked

"Your majesty, the baby, the baby..." she kept repeating.

The Queen grabbed her and shook her.

"What about the baby?" she shouted.

"The baby... has been changed." Then the servant started to cry.

The Queen found the baby still asleep in the royal cradle. But it was not the infant of the night before. He was *nivuru nivuru*, black as the blackest night.

The Queen was desperate: all the houses in the kingdom were searched to find real prince, but he was nowhere to be found. Sages were called from surrounding counties, but they did not know what to do. Believing it to be a curse, the guards were sent to search for the old Nona everywhere, but to no avail. The King held the crying Queen, and spoke.

"Our son or not, this baby will be baptized tomorrow."

No one was around on the morning of the baptism. In the Church of Saint Agatha, the priest took the baby from the arms of the King, and only a few servants were present to assist the Queen, who was very weak. Carefully holding the baby, the priest submerged his head quickly in the baptismal font.

"*Ego te baptizo in nomine patris, et filii, et spiritus sancti.*" The priest recited.

"Amen!" Everybody said.

The baby cried, and his hair, wet from the holy water, was blond once more. The Priest marveled at this, and dipping his stole in the holy water, used it to rub the baby's skin, which at each stroke turned milky white.'

Maria would always question this part, asking where the original baby was hiding, or arguing that nothing bad had really happened. The baby just got dirty and the holy water washed it all away. Her mother would smile patiently, caressing her head. She would hear the story again and again, variation on the motif of the *figghiu cangiatu*. Babies disappeared, then magically reappeared, washed of their parents' sins. They came out clean in the end, pale as she had always been, and as sinless. The good, quiet one. The virgin librarian. What a sad cliché. Somewhere, in a dark corner, in an attic, under old curtains and boxes of china, something lay in wait. Something had always been there, perhaps before she had. She wondered if her father's eyes had seen what was there, if they had been seeing it for all his life.

The man next to her stood up and disappeared behind a door, as directed by the man on the phone. The door had milky white glass; people went in but seldom came out. Then the man on the phone nodded to her, pointed to another door, almost identical to the first.

In the small office, a man of indefinite age was sitting, his jacket carefully hanging from the backrest of the chair, his tie loose.

'We'll need to ask some questions,' he said.

Maria nodded.

'Please state your name for the record.'

But she just shook her head, holding back the tears.

From Castlebar to Dundalk
By Bernadette Klubb

The Pope was coming. His Holiness, Pope John Paul II, was touching down in Knock Airport that very night and from the coast of Antrim all the way down to Dingle Bay, there was talk of nothing else.

Elaine Goss had been at her sewing machine for two weeks solid, and like Julie Andrews with her curtains in *The Sound of Music*, had produced five spanking new outfits from scraps and oddments for her brood to wear at the big parade in three days' time.

The pile of religious paraphernalia on the sideboard grew: candles, rosary beads, holy pictures stacked like a deck of cards, all destined to accompany Elaine and her children to the papal blessing on the steps of the cathedral on Sunday. Eventually, each of these items would become a trophy in the religious treasuries of this or that family member who could not attend in person for some reason - although *what possible reason* that might be, the woman was at a total loss to imagine.

And there was the rub, thought Elaine, mashing the pedal of the old Singer machine, the fly in the papal unction. No matter that the name-calling was confined to her head for the sake of the wee ones, the mental hurl of abuse was some small relief at least, the object of the abuse being that half-heathen (only half?) self-gratifying excuse for a husband who had swept her up the same cathedral aisle a decade before. Now *there* was a man who could come up with possible reasons to take himself off to the other side of the country at the drop of a hat.

In spite of her anger, a ghost of regret stole into her red-rimmed eyes as they inspected the mini yellow and white flags she was finishing for the children to wave. She regretted her bitter "Don't bother coming back!" as he drove off that morning once the children had been dispatched to school.

The wreck, a Spanish galleon of some significance, that Eamon Goss was going to dive on with his cousins James and Rory, had shifted on the seabed off the west coast of Ireland. By Eamon's reckoning, the majority of the diving fraternity would not even hear about it until after the Holy Father was done blessing the good folk of all four provinces and the local news was again scrabbling for something other than 'the Troubles' to report. The men planned to arrive ahead of the Vatican visitors. They would be first to the nationals with the newest photos of the famous vessel's foundering bones. As for old John P, well, he was sure he would understand. They said he was a working-class man himself, didn't they?

Climbing into his drysuit, waiting for one of his cousins to help him with the weights and safety harness, he recalled his wife's face from that morning - flustered, angry, hurt. A seed of guilt cracked, albeit in the very infertile soil of his *perfectly possible reason* for not being there. After all, when most of your work involved dragging industrial rubbish and the occasional suicide from clogged up canals and polluted urban waterways, the chance of earning a few quid from a dip in the Atlantic was surely as good for the soul as yet another sung mass.

Only, he regretted having risen to Elaine's girlish dismissal. The bitterness curdled his voice unnaturally, the words meant nothing, less than that, a stock response: "Don't worry, I won't!" Don't come back, indeed. Sure what would she do without him? Ack, she would forget about it all in the kaleidoscope of the papal high jinks. He would be home on Monday after all the hullabaloo was done. They'd be grand.

Aside from Eamon's diving suit and weights, the only equipment required was photographic and they had no more than a morning's work ahead, all told. Consequently, the boat they hired was on the small side, neat. Even so, clearing the ladder to deck, Rory had to turn through a full three hundred and sixty degrees before belief was forced upon him. The small, neat deck, tidy, was completely empty of human form. He yelled for James to 'get the fuck up here!' The deck remained defiantly tidy. The helmet of Eamon's diving suit sat squarely in the 'V' of the bow, the safety harness lay off to the side, still coiled, the canvas pack of weights, still unopened. The waves slapped the odd white eddy high enough to splash through the lowest rails. The Atlantic was having a peaceful day and its careless undulations, like the deck, presented a tidy, neat and empty surface to the world.

'It was sunny, calm,' Rory would tell the Gardaí lamely when he was taking their statements in Castlebar's one-man police station.

'He just wasn't there. Not on the boat, not in the sea,' James would shake his head.

Drowning is not a fragrant business. Not even when the deceased is considerate enough to show up on a beach within the hour, and not a mile from the spot where he had left the neat, clueless deck of the hired boat.

'*Dundalk?*' The undertaker in Castlebar wondered should he go for the calculator or the embalming fluid first. It was unfortunate that the calculator won.

The undertaker apologised if he appeared mercenary but he had to allow for the traffic, the extra mileage to avoid the traffic, the extra staff who would be required to accompany them - they would need to, you know, 'tidy up' the deceased again at journey's end...if the men really could not be dissuaded from beginning the long road home until...

His widow was distraught, said James, and no, she would not wait for the Holy Father's departure.

Finally, a deal was struck, a bottle of Black Bush was opened (maybe two) and it was entirely possible, Rory was to confess to one of the mourners the following day outside the wake house, that the undertaker and his sons were somewhat less than thorough when it came to the actual embalming.

'What with all the calculating of routes and diversions y'understand, I don't know where they got the time to lay him out at all', was what he said, avoiding direct reference to the growing ripeness in the air, for he had no wish to speak ill of the dead who, after all, could no longer be held responsible for their own personal hygiene.

The swooning mourner was less deferential and complained readily that she 'knew Eamon was home before the hearse was in the street,' and that sniff was definitely loaded with inference rather than grief.

Neither Rory, James nor any of the cross-country undertaking retinue would have argued with that. They had snailed their way, a handful of funeral cars playing some machiavellian game of tag with the rest of the population – a.k.a the papal procession. Where they could, they skirted the advancing crowds, arching randomly northwards or southwards in search of lighter traffic. All they achieved was almost doubling what started out as a two hundred mile journey, and by lunchtime, on one of the hottest days in September 1979, the undertaker and his sons were doing shifts of no more than thirty minutes each.

In the end, the Pope and Eamon Goss had reached their respective Dundalk destinations at more or less the same time - one in a haze of incense and one in the pall of his recent, salty demise.

Elaine had put away the children's *Sound of Music* clothes and pressed their school uniforms instead. The boys suitably solemn in grey, just a flash of gold and red in the black ties, and the girls wore their dark brown winter gymslips in spite of the weather. One way or another, the whole town baked.

'You couldn'a made it up!' Sissy Dunn told her sister in America the following week. 'It went from bad to worse when the *local* undertaker turned up to collect the chief mourners. He musta got mixed up with something to do with the Pope and up they landed in thon new white saloon they bought for weddings. Would you credit it?'

'The saddest thing was the wee one of course. Losing your Da is nasty business at the best of times, but the poor child was retching on the smell in the chapel and when that arsehole Murphy (may God forgive me) and him only fresh out of the seminary (don't start me on the priests) tried to tell her it had something to do with her poor drowned Da, well she just kicked him in the shins, hard, and then smart as you like, stuck her wee yellow and white flag that her Ma had let her hang on to, right up his nostril!'

Elaine had not even scolded the child. Alone in a chapel of jumpy mourners - all that coughing, people coming and going, hovering near the doors - she remained oblivious to the smell.

She was thinking about all the people, nurses, train drivers - there were loads of them when you thought about it, who had *perfectly possible reasons* for not being somewhere. Just ordinary folk, out there, grabbing the chance to earn a few quid.

Fred Fletcher
By Matthew Louis

Having scrubbed his hands a second time so he wouldn't have to hear how disgusting they were, Fred dropped down at his kitchen table and sighed. Clarissa, getting out the articles to make him a sandwich, spoke into the refrigerator.

'A man named Cliff O'Sullivan called and said he wanted to come by and see you. I told him to call back tonight.' She flung Fred a quick look. 'He didn't have very good manners.'

Fred said, 'Oh yeah?' and blinked a couple of times. He felt as if a confusion of angry bees was closing around his head. He felt his lips mashing together and his chest filling up and hardening like a compressor tank. He wanted to hammer the table with his fist and let his face contort in misery; he wanted to lurch across the kitchen and roar his frustration at a volume that would make Clarissa melt to the floor and leave her trembling beside the stainless steel dishwasher.

But she had her back to him, busily manufacturing his sandwich. He stared at her trim little hips and slowly expelled air through his nostrils. Shit, he thought, nothing but a full confession will do... A full confession! During his half hour lunch break? To his pregnant wife? To this hardheaded prissy bitch? No, no, he loved Clarissa, she was everything. She would understand but he would have to break it to her properly. He tried to get his thoughts in order.

The goddamned O'Sullivans had never been able to hold their alcohol. That was the first point to get across. You get those people drunk and they were likely to force themselves on their own sisters or set fire to the Presbyterian Church. And, well, why try to put a nice face on it? They were like rabid animals when they were sober. They were white trash. You put them all in a gas chamber and you'd be improving the human race.

Fred kept his face placid. On the off-white, delicately embroidered tablecloth in front of him he twirled a piece of blue pocket-lint between stained thumb and forefinger. It had been more than ten years since he'd left Deer Run, the small Oregon town he was from, and he had managed to banish the O'Sullivans from his consciousness. Now, in just the manner he would expect them to, they stomped and tumbled obnoxiously back into the forefront of his thoughts. He could see them now in his mind's eye as plainly as if they had followed him here and were standing under the grape arbor outside the window.

The whole bunch of them, the women and the men, looked alike. They were all tall and rangy and homely, and they unvaryingly had crooked teeth and cruel little pig's eyes. Fred knew they had indeed married outside their clan. There was some Korinskys in there, and some Hauses, he remembered, but to look at any of the couples in the group, and the clusters of scruffy children they produced like bad ideas, you would think they were not so much a family as some sort of distinct species.

He snorted at his thoughts then flicked his eyes toward Clarissa. She was slicing cheese on the cutting board.

How to make her understand? The sons of bitches were mean. And not just mean but vicious. If you wound up on the other side in one of their countless feuds, you could expect four or five lanky, ugly, snarling O'Sullivans to try to catch you somewhere alone. And if they caught you, you could be sure they wouldn't allow you any fighting chance, but would be swinging two-by-fours or trying to flay you with bicycle chains.

But Clarissa didn't have an inkling about people like this. She thought that real white trash didn't actually exist – that they were just some 'type,' some gag invented by scriptwriters and TV comedians. And if she didn't understand this, how could he explain the rest to her?

Okay, Fred thought bluntly, I'm a murderer. It boils down to that. But I only killed one of them. He grimaced. He shouldn't insult the guy's memory, he thought. Leonard O'Sullivan hadn't been that bad.

He just wished he'd been honest about this before. But he wasn't sure Clarissa would understand – in fact, he had always been sure she wouldn't. He had been acquitted, and the incident had been chalked up to a drunken tragedy, but the subject had always seemed impossible even to think about in her presence.

'Here you are,' Clarissa said in a slight sing-song as she set down the ham sandwich. It was, to Fred, an exotic looking item, made with dark, grainy whole wheat, with crisp, organic lettuce peeking out, and placed with geometric precision on the salmon colored plate. There was a small pile of sweet pickle chips (healthier than potato chips) sitting in the neat triangle between the sandwich halves. The whole thing looked like it was waiting to be photographed.

Fred said, 'Thanks honey,' in the blandest voice he could manage. He carefully avoided looking into her face

But her hand was suddenly under his chin, tilting his head back, 'You okay, Freddy? Your face is all flushed. Are you coming down with something?'

'Uh,' he cleared his throat, 'Maybe. I don't think so.' His face remained up when her hand pulled away.

'Is that guy, what's-his-name – O'Sullivan? – somebody to you? You haven't said a word since I mentioned him.'

Fred raised his eyebrows and looked into Clarissa's incredible, perpetually startled brown eyes for a moment, then said, 'No! What was his name? O'Sullivan? No! I never heard of him!'

*

As he drove his tiny Honda back to the shop, Fred both regretted the bold-faced lie and felt heroic for keeping the mess contained within his own mind. Clarissa wouldn't get it. She loved him, and she would probably stand by him at this point, being pregnant and all, but she may never feel the same again if he told her. And if she did leave him, if all this fell apart, where would Fred Fletcher be?

A large part of the attraction – hell, all of the attraction – was that Clarissa was the kind of girl Fred couldn't normally get. She was petite and beautiful and built like a gazelle, and he felt like he'd won the lottery. It was true that she was three years older than him, and she had confessed early in their relationship, just so all the cards were on the table, that after dating real assholes throughout her twenties she had wised up and begun keeping an eye out for a guy just like him; a guy she could settle down and start a family with; a good, hardworking (short) guy. A (short) guy who wouldn't have girls tempting him away from her at every turn – a guy she could trust.

And all this was okay because he figured he was getting, by far, the better end of the deal. Here was little Freddy Fletcher from Deer Run, Oregon, married to this phenomenal, gorgeous little dynamo. Clarissa kept the house as neat and charming as a Holiday Inn lobby, she was a great cook (even if he hadn't eaten a hamburger in a year) and she made a very deliberate point of, well, servicing him regularly. And she accepted him for what he was – a mechanic was a noble enough trade. But she had finally sort of herded him down to the local junior college, and pretty soon he would have his degree in business administration, and then her father was going to loan them a little more money so they could start some kind of business of their own. Fred had been daydreaming of his own garage with all Snap-On tools, twin hydraulic lifts, and a tow truck fully outfitted for expensive roadside repairs, but Clarissa was already keeping a tentative eye on storefronts for lease in town so she could have her antique shop. He guessed it would be fun to learn about antiques.

As he nudged his way through the lunchtime traffic his mind constructed the glittery image of himself: Fred Fletcher, a fine proud citizen complete with beautiful wife, new child, and his own business. The thought was terrifying. It made him feel like the most obscene sort of imposter. Why, he wondered, hadn't he ever told Clarissa about his past? And his mind answered: because she would have made polite excuses, canceled your next date, and never talked to you again. It was true. She wanted a clean, respectable, stalwart little man who she could (might as well admit it) remake according to her tastes. As he listened to his turn indicator click-clacking and waited to make the left-hand turn into Curly's Auto Repair, he felt like weeping. He wanted like hell to be that man; or rather, to remain that man.

*

On his break, smoking a cigarette with black hands behind the garage, Fred couldn't clear his head. He looked vacantly at his left fist where a radiant, glistening, red wedge of exposed meat leapt out from the coating of grease. He hadn't had a stupid knucklebuster like that in years, but, goddamnit, his mind was gone today. It was just unfair. He felt like he'd been plunged back into his seedy past, like the cobwebs of his awful, backward youth in Deer Run were clinging all over him for everyone to see.

His mind wanted to go there. He had to face it. This thing with Clarissa was a fantasy. Underneath it all he was still that idiot kid who wasn't sure what the word ambition meant. He had to accept the reality, because Cliff O'Sullivan (which one was he? Fred wasn't sure) had come out here like some desperado in a spaghetti western, and he meant to teach Freddy Fletcher and the world a lesson.

Aw the hell, Fred thought. I did it, didn't I?

And now he stared at the vacant lot next to Curly's, and he was back there, in Deer Run. He was nineteen but nobody checked IDs on the locals. He was walking into Buzz'z Tavern, already pretty well drunk, and there was Leonard O'Sullivan, swaying in front of the bar, tossing off shots of Jack Daniels.

The thing was, Leonard O'Sullivan was the single member of the clan who was all right. He was quiet and pleasant. Everyone in town liked him and agreed he was a bright kid. He had even been caught on several occasions with his nose in a book. At the trial the startling fact would come out that Leonard had never actually been drunk before.

Fred had stepped to the bar and Leonard's inspired voice had blown against him like shrapnel: 'Why Fred Fletcher! You dirty, cocksucking, grease-eating little son of a bitch!' Fred and Leonard had always been mutually respectful, and he was not at any sort of odds with the rest of

112

the O'Sullivans, so he narrowed his eyes and said nothing – waited for the big idea to be made plain to him. Two other O'Sullivans had been nearby, giggling and elbowing each other in a congratulatory fashion, exactly as youths do when they induce the family dog to drink beer and then watch it bumble around the yard.

Leonard had then grinned dreamily and pressed his long face toward Fred and said, 'I don't care if yer a true-to-life bastard, Fred! An' I don't care if yer a little goddamned squirt either! I like you! I always have!'

The desperate laughter of the other two O'Sullivans tickled Fred's ears like glass raining down on concrete and he felt the muscles of his shoulders and back bunch up against each other. It was well known in town that Fred Fletcher was fatherless, and he was still too young to have come to terms with his height of five feet, four inches.

Then Leonard had slouched into Fred's space and draped an arm over his shoulders, calling out, 'Aye! Tim! Get a shot for my friend Fred Fletcher, the famous unclaimed bastard pigmy of Deer Run!' Now the other O'Sullivans were falling off their stools, howling, clutching each other, and digging tears from their eyes.

Fred Fletcher was strong. He was already a brilliant mechanic at nineteen and he'd been employed at that point maintaining a small fleet of diesel trucks for a local outfit called Springbrook. His arms were engorged with muscle from manhandling the oversized engine parts and straining against the torque wrenches. So when his anger swept him up and his eyes suddenly popped wide and he hurled his elbow at Leonard O'Sullivan's face, it was with unusual force.

Everyone in town knew that Leonard O'Sullivan was an epileptic – many people had witnessed his quaking 'grand mal' seizures – but this bit of trivia was the last thing on Fred's mind. His elbow struck Leonard's nose with vicious impact and the young man went over backward and hit the grimy floorboards like a thing that had never been alive. Having thus dispensed with one of them, Fred leapt over Leonard and set himself to the badly-conceived task of destroying the other two O'Sullivans.

Several minutes later, when the combatants were finally pried apart and Fred was held by two men in such a way that his feet swiped embarrassingly above the floor, someone had said, 'Heeey! Something's wrong with this guy!' And motion had slowed for Fred until it seemed to grind to stillness. He had gaped down for an eternity of seconds at Leonard O'Sullivan, feeling reality become strangely disjointed. Leonard was on his back, wide-eyed, with his hands curled into claws at his sides and his face a hideous, bruised, impossible shade of blue. Fred would always recall that square, hairy, pink hand closing around Leonard's cheeks, shifting the face side to side. Then the gruff, quiet voice saying, 'This fucking guy's dead!'

It had been the best thing that ever happened to Fred. It had gotten him out of Deer Run. He had been acquitted of all charges – the public defender argued convincingly that Leonard O'Sullivan died as a result of an epileptic seizure and nothing more; and furthermore, who could really say that the seizure wasn't already in progress when Fred struck? And, to get down to brass tacks, wasn't the alcohol really the lethal factor? If anyone was responsible for Leonard's death, the lawyer concluded, it was none other than the poor boy's own reckless, irresponsible cousins.

Fred was set free after a stern talking-to from the judge. Within a week he had returned to his former life and might have lived out the rest of it in Deer Run, but a month later, when he had scrambled out of Don Padre's and been chased down Main Street by four O'Sullivans and only escaped by hurling himself through the doors of the police station, he began to think about moving. Then, when he had been driving his pickup over the 142 on his way to work and a bullet had caused the rear window to explode around his head, he had hunched against the steering wheel, picked up speed, and said through clenched teeth that that was it. He was moving away and he wasn't telling anyone where he was going.

'Hey! What the hell, Freddy!' He looked up, startled. Curly himself, big and smudged, with his beer gut inflating the middle of his coveralls, was scowling down at Fred, 'You still work here or what?!'

*

Nothing happened. Cliff O'Sullivan was a wash. Fred went home from work, showered, ate Clarissa's lasagna and salad, watched two hours of reality TV and drank two glasses of red wine.

As the wine worked he began to feel so good that he wanted to tell Clarissa the whole story just so he could celebrate his continuing success and bright future. The idea that his past would somehow find him here after all this time became more ridiculous every time it crossed his mind. Life was still grand and he was still the luckiest man on earth.

Clarissa looked at him coquettishly and repeatedly asked him why he was smiling like he was. He watched her drink three and then four glasses of wine and they both knew where the evening was going and Fred felt, once again, like he'd won the lottery.

*

They made love on the couch. They pursued the act dutifully, clenching and unclenching together like workmates quietly laboring to complete a well-practiced procedure. Fred recognized by the moans and the liveliness of her hips that Clarissa had begun spiraling up toward orgasm and he increased the intensity of his onslaught accordingly. They had muted the television with a hasty manipulation of the remote control and now he surreptitiously eyed her in the flickering light, picking up his cues from the degree of contortion on her small face. It was one of the good ones. Her being pregnant, they didn't have to think about protection and with no such distractions things had progressed perfectly. He had now caught her rhythm and he just had to keep mashing into her, on time, and soon she would be his. His arms were folded beneath her narrow, sinuous back and one hand was clamped on the nape of her neck – as if he'd had to wrestle her into this position. He felt himself beginning to boil also and –

The phone on the end table assaulted the room with its shocking, unrestrained, electronic holler.

Their motion ceased. Fred drew back and stared into Clarissa's face.

He fixed his eyes on the square green digits glowing on the VCR: 11:24. The phone unleashed another prolonged, idiotic, pulsating bleep, scattering the last wisps of their sex-spell. 'What the hell,' Fred muttered. Clarissa had already shifted and worked herself upright. She reached over the couch-arm and snatched the phone up midway through the third ring.

'Hello?' Her face had already returned to its keen, female sensibilities. 'Ye-es?' she sounded at once uncertain and annoyed. The skin between her eyebrows creased and her eyes, big and glassy in the television light, swiveled up to meet Fred's. She covered the mouth-piece and breathed, 'It's that guy that called today... '

Fred's heart stumbled. He cleared his throat and lifted the phone from her hand, 'Hello?'

The voice was a deep, flat, unnerving monotone: 'Time to pay the piper, Freddy! I'll see you tomorrow! Semper fi!' Fred opened his mouth to respond but there was a gentle click and he was left perched over Clarissa, holding the dead receiver stupidly against his head.

*

The next morning Fred pulled out of the driveway and drove to work in a state of torment. He felt as if the very fibers of his being were tearing and the larger shreds of himself remained in the house with Clarissa. He had bags under his eyes, he had shaved hastily and cut himself three times, and he compulsively mussed his hair as he thought about his situation.

They had never completed their lovemaking but had had a long, long talk instead, and Fred had done almost all of the talking. He had told her everything and she had taken it in wordlessly, obviously acutely displeased. She had said almost nothing but her silence and her expression made it plain that she felt cheated: that Fred was a liar, that he had married her under false pretenses, and that this was his problem and she expected him to make it go away. They had agreed, however, that if any strange men came to the door Clarissa wouldn't open it, and if there were any more calls today she would immediately contact the police.

Fred prayed that it wouldn't come to that. Once the police were involved the fiasco would somehow be official. The black and white cruiser in front of the house, advertising their dilemma to the neighborhood, the reports to be made, and worst of all, some young, burr-headed officer being in control of the situation—assuming the role of alpha male while Fred stood by, a model of uselessness.

At work Fred had asked Curly what 'semper fi' meant, (the alien words had been whirling around inside his skull all night) and Curly had informed him it was something Marines chanted, some Latin thing that meant 'from many, one' he thought.

At the word 'Marines,' the dam containing Fred's horror had cracked and begun bleeding out all over his consciousness again. His idea of a Marine was a big, skin-headed, muscular kid with a loud manner and sort of intense, empty eyes: a killing machine. The thought of one of these animals cross-breeding with one of the O'Sullivans – and the resultant monster wanting him dead – was too awful to contemplate.

'Jesus, Freddy, you look green. You alright?'

Inspiration struck. 'No,' Fred said weakly, 'I was up sick all night, I've got some kind of stomach virus. I think maybe I better go home.'

'She-yit!' Curly said. 'I knew something was wrong soon as I saw you! Well, if you're sick, you're sick. Listen, just put that radiator back in that old Dodge for me and then take off. I'll see if Tony can come in this afternoon.'

*

Clarissa didn't ask him why he was home. She skewered him on her gaze, extended her arm toward him, and asked 'Is this the boy you killed?'

He lifted his hand slowly and accepted the 4-by-6, matt-finish school photograph. It was a twenty-year-old picture of an ugly adolescent boy. It was Leonard O'Sullivan. He had a dopey smile on an outsized mouth and large, staggered, front teeth. His innocent blue eyes beckoned to the world, his long, narrow face stirred the dust in a dark corner of Fred's mind. The boy's hair was a disordered, dishwater-blonde mullet cut, his shirt a faded, frayed, plaid flannel. This homely little artifact was a window back into those few square miles that comprised Deer Run and those long, shameful years that comprised Fred's youth. He looked up from the picture. His voice came out slightly shrill: 'Where'd you get this?'

Clarissa told him. She had heard the lid thunk on the door-side mailbox. She had heard an engine rev and a car drive away. She had found this picture sitting in the box by itself: this sad, dead kid smiling in the darkness.

'That man's around somewhere!' Clarissa accused. 'He's probably watching the house right now, waiting for you to leave. I'm calling the police!'

'No!' Fred stepped toward Clarissa as she stepped toward the phone. His abrupt action implied that he would physically stop her if need be. He was surprised by the vehemence of his own response and immediately tried to make up ground. 'I'll solve this,' he said, then placated her with, 'I'll just wait and when the guy shows up, I'll deal with him. That's why I came home from work.'

'Good,' Clarissa's tone and posture became haughty, 'I'm going to Lisa's for the day. You can call me when it's solved.'

'Good,' Fred responded, but something in his mind snapped as gently and quietly as a small bone; his face twisted into a sneer and he was astonished to hear himself spit, 'Leave, bitch.'

Clarissa spun and glared at him. She could not have looked more stunned if Fred had belted her in the mouth. The diminutive, mild-mannered mechanic had never had such a lapse of manners since they had known each other, but he felt no remorse. He was functioning on almost no sleep, he had a vengeful Marine circling him like a hawk, and the person who was supposed to support him in good times and bad was introducing a blare of static into his already reeling mind.

'That's it, Fred!' said Clarissa, and turned on her heel and stalked off toward their bedroom. Fred made a face and repeated in snotty, nasal tones, 'That's it, Fred,' as he dragged his Mr. Coffee to the front of the counter.

*

He sat on the front stoop, crowded and tickled by Clarissa's hanging plants and potted plants and her small jungle of ferns, irises, rhododendrons, bleeding hearts and other exotic foliage that she cultivated in front of the house to impress the neighborhood. He slurped at his coffee, wincing as it scorched his lips and tongue but willing the caffeine to enter his veins and energize his muscles and brain. Before him the stately trees of Martin Drive laid long, pretty shadows across the street and the modern, Craftsman-style houses stood in a row, nestled amid vibrant green landscaping, stunningly handsome with their flawless paint jobs and complimentary trim. Fred could not help but love the sight of his street in the morning.

Clarissa seemed to be taking her time leaving and, goddamnit, he wanted her gone so he could do this. He thought of marching into the house, seizing her arm, and conducting her to her car, but she would probably call the police on him if he did such a thing.

Maybe it was all over, Fred thought, and he felt his throat constricting at the possibility. His own quaint residence mocked him. What did he have to do with this luxuriant emerald lawn neatly striped by the wheels of the Mexican gardener's mower? What did he have to do with this new house with the ultra-modern black trim (who had ever heard of black trim!) and the blooming flowers and the window boxes drooling pretty plants, and Clarissa's sleek BMW in the driveway? Of course it galled Cliff O'Sullivan (whichever one of them he was) to see little Freddy Fletcher here, playing the role of upper-middle class suburban asshole.

The sound of a monstrous engine wafted up the street and Fred became motionless. It was the inverse of what one usually heard in this neighborhood, where the more silent a car was, the better it was assumed to be. The engine glugged and pitched to a higher, more urgent growl. Fred cocked his head and judged it to be a Chevy, no doubt about 400

119

cubic inches, and unquestionably a V-8... The Malibu careened into view. It was clearly its owner's pride and joy – the sort of vehicle that is a work forever in progress. The car was a racy yellow with cheap, self-apply window tint giving it a deliberately sinister look. It was crouched on meaty, glossy black tires, with square patches of gray primer sown all over it – covering where rust-holes had been cut out and repaired. It rumbled past, and the driver – oh yes, he had an elongated, narrow, mean face with a pair of mirrored aviator sunglasses clapped in place under his brow ridges – the driver turned his head as he eased past, locking gazes with Fred, and then... he... smiled. But it wasn't a smile as much a chimpanzee-like baring of the teeth. It said, 'Now I've got you where I want you and I'm gonna enjoy destroying you.'

The car glided out of view but Fred listened as it circled around and then he heard the engine being fed gasoline, hammering its cylinders up to a throaty roar, and he saw the car again, an affront to the entire neighborhood, rocketing up the center of the street, coming right at the rear corner of Fred's Honda. It leapt forward in a show of ludicrous, macho belligerence and then the brakes engaged at the last possible moment, the fat tires shrieking briefly as the Malibu lurched to sudden stillness in front of the house. The engine chugged a moment and then died.

Fred stood up on the landing in the hope of looking taller. He tried to sip his coffee casually, but his hand was rattling so badly that it sloshed onto the front of his mechanic's shirt.

Cliff O'Sullivan stood from his car. His large, golden-haired, crew-cut head rose a good two feet over the Malibu's roof. He removed his sunglasses, bent at the waist, and set them on the dashboard. He walked around the hood of his car with his small eyes – looking as if they'd been installed by a taxidermist – aimed at Fred.

He was, to Fred's mind, the quintessential Marine. His jaw was perfectly shaven; he was dressed in khaki pants and a white T-shirt that clung to the curvatures of his well-exercised torso. His arms were bent so the elbows angled out neatly on either side, and his walk – his very walk – was robotic. A machine was what he was, and he had been programmed – or programmed himself – to seek out and destroy Fred Fletcher.

Fred said, 'Cliff!' and then he cleared his throat and deepened his voice, 'Cliff! Let's talk about this thing!'

The robot halted five feet away. Fred, standing as he was, raised a full twelve inches on the landing, was eye-to-eye with the man. Cliff's face hung slack except where one nostril twitched with what could become a sneer.

'That was a long time ago, Cliff. I was just a kid!'

Cliff spoke: 'You got off scot-free.' It was either laughable or it was terrifying – his voice was a deep, affected, mechanical monotone. 'You killed my brother in cold blood – '

'It was an accident!'

' – and now – '

'Did you hear me? I didn't mean to!'

' – I'm gonna even up.'

'What's it gonna solve?' Fred practically screamed the question, gesturing in the air with his free hand.

Cliff O'Sullivan flexed his jaws. The blue of his eyes was liquid with shadowy reflections. He narrowed his gaze and reported in his dead voice: 'Lenny was tutoring me, I was gonna go to college. I didn't even end up going to high school. Momma got depressed – she's in a home now. Daddy got locked up. Instead of college I joined the Corps and now I got this Gulf War Syndrome... All of it 'cause you killed Lenny.'

Fred wished like hell he'd let Clarissa call the police. This was not even a remotely rational person. This man had constructed an alternate reality wherein Fred Fletcher was the wellspring of every bad thing that had ever happened to him and his family. Fred did a quick calculation and knew he couldn't get in the front door before the O'Sullivan would be upon him. He did another calculation and knew that his coffee, if he dashed it into the man's face, wasn't hot enough to make a difference. He sighed, was swept up in another wave of furious exasperation, and said, 'Alright, Cliff. Let's do it.'

Before he could think about his actions he had hopped off the landing and strode into the middle of the front lawn. He tossed his half-full coffee cup harmlessly onto the grass. His hands closed and opened, closed and opened, and the lumpy, enormous muscles of his forearms bunched and smoothed, bunched and smoothed. Why he glanced toward the house he didn't know, but there was Clarissa, standing like a ghost in the picture window behind the planter box... just... watching them. He felt miniature. Inadequate. He saw himself through Clarissa's eyes and he knew he must look like a ten year old, juxtaposed as he was to this rawboned giant. He felt defeated before they had so much as touched one another.

Cliff O'Sullivan had assumed some kind of martial arts stance and he worked his way toward his opponent in a sidelong shuffle. Fred was intensely conscious of the wild spectacle they presented to anyone who might look: two latter-day gladiators facing off in on a lovely spring morning, their arena a plush dark lawn on a quiet street in an upscale neighborhood.

They crashed into each other, they threw their fists, they clawed and grappled and went over together and rolled and clutched desperately on the soft grass. Fred felt the point of a finger pressing into his eye socket. He felt knuckles jolting his head. He felt his insides jar sickeningly with blows to his ribcage. He swung blindly, over and over, aiming for the jaw, the cheekbone, the nose. He gained the advantage, crawled atop of his adversary and rained down deadly blows with his right fist: Thud! Thud! Thud! Thud! The punches were landing with gratifying impact but he suddenly caught himself. His fist floated over his head but didn't descend. Something was wrong. The eyes were open, the mouth lay sideways, the nostrils were blooming with red blood, and the man didn't move. Fred waited. His heart had become unmoored and was now lodged in the bottom of his throat, convulsing explosively. Panic began to consume him like rising flames. He groped clumsily at O'Sullivan's long neck, pushing his fingertips into the flesh next to the prodigious Adam's apple and... Nothing!

'Clarissa!' He raised his voice, 'Clarissa!' He could hardly get the words out. 'Call an ambulance!' he sobbed, 'Hurry!'

*

A woodpecker beat its face on a tree somewhere and other birds could be heard arguing around Clarissa's feeder. The morning sun pressed against the curtains so the living room was aglow with placid light. Fred Jr. looked up at his father and formed what was almost a true smile. Fred smiled back with genuine pleasure and worked the nipple of the bottle into his son's mouth. He was actually better than Clarissa at getting the child to take all of his milk. He gently tilted the cylinder and propped it at exactly the right angle and watched as the tiny hands fell into position on either side of it. He was also adept at calming Fred Jr. during crying fits, and he was a very efficient diaper changer (after a short term of adjustment he didn't even mind the messes produced by such an uncorrupted digestive system). He was alone with the baby every day from 5AM, when Fred Jr. tended to wake up, until 8AM when Clarissa tended to wake up. Then Fred passed the child off, showered, shaved slowly and thoroughly, dressed in loafers, slacks and a conservative-yet-casual button down shirt, and drove downtown in his glossy Toyota Avalon to open Found Treasures Antiques.

He seldom thought about the grotesque scandal of the previous year. The buzzwords – collapsed windpipe, self-defense, innocent verdict – summarized the story and he never needed to revisit it in any greater detail. The incident had, however, shocked Clarissa into a state of awe and respectfulness and had therefore brought them closer together and solidified their relationship. Fred always fought the notion down before it could become a conscious thought, but for this reason he wouldn't trade the experience for anything – even the lives of the two poor, pathetic O'Sullivans. Clarissa was all his now and he had walked through fire to claim her and –

The phone on the end table assaulted the room with its shocking, unrestrained, electronic holler. Fred Jr. started and then suckled at his bottle with renewed concentration. Fred freed a hand and snatched up the phone before it could ring again and half whispered, 'Hello?'

The voice was a cretinous, back-country hiss, 'You think that's the end of it? You think you can just kill Cliffy and go on with your life like nothing happened?'

For The Taking
By Anne Leigh Parrish

Angie needed a drink, and had already waited ten minutes for Fran to offer her one. Finally she went into the kitchen, found a glass, and returned to the living room. She joined Fran on the soft leather couch, and helped herself to the whiskey from the crystal bottle on the coffee table.

The funeral had been long. A lot of people Angie didn't know gave voice to her father's good deeds, *I remember when he taught Bess to play her first scale*, and *he guided Collin through his first recital*. Fran was the last to speak. She cried as she described their seven lovely years together – *a second marriage for us both but even better than the first* – then closed with *your music is silent now, my love, though for you my ear remains keen.*

To Angie it was big bore. She'd given up on her father years before, and was only there to get something for her trouble, something she could take away and hang onto.

'Find out about insurance,' Kevin had said as Angie boarded the bus to Ann Arbor. 'An old guy like that, he'd have insurance.' He didn't, though. He didn't have a will, either.

'Because he wasn't planning to die,' said Fran, when Angie asked why not. 'Don't you think he'd have put his affairs in order, otherwise?'

Angie sipped her drink. Her father was only sixty-two. He'd been a piano teacher. Angie's mother had been one of his students. Their marriage was four months older than Angie, a last minute arrangement, she was always told. Angie was five when her mother ran off with another man, and she remembered nothing of it, though her father said she'd been right there, watching the car drive away. What Angie did remember was her mother's absence, the sudden silence in the house, and then a postcard from Montana saying, I made a mistake. Her mother didn't write again, she didn't come home, and went on living with her mistake, Angie hoped, until word came of her death from pneumonia in an Arizona hospital three years later.

'There are a few photo albums you can have, and some costume jewelry of your mother's, although I don't know why he kept it, under the circumstances. Oh, and you can take the ashtrays. You know how he loved those,' said Fran.

And the bars he lifted them from, with Angie on the look-out, those many nights when staying home was no comfort at all.

In the beginning they were turned away. *What are you thinking, trying to bring a child in here?* In time they were allowed to stay. And stay they did, through the lunch crowd, the after lunch crowd, the happy hour crowd, smoke and laughter taking them towards night. *Everything I ever learned, I learned in a bar,* Angie had told Kevin more than once.

What she learned was how to use silence and wide eyes to get pretzels and soda, sometimes a sandwich, sometimes a sweater or a pair of shoes that no longer fit the bartender's son or daughter. People gave you what they thought you needed easily enough. The trick was getting what you wanted.

'What about that old piano?' Angie asked Fran.

'The one in storage? Goodness, I'd forgotten all about it.'

Angie's father discovered it in the basement of a church where he'd woken up after walking the streets and screaming at the violet sky. Angie had spent the same night alone in their drafty house, with only the television's grey-blue face for company. Later, at the church, she held her father's sweaty hand, thought of how hungry she was, and looked at the piano. Tiny painted roses decorated the closed keyboard lid. The finish was dull and scratched, something her father pointed out while he haggled with the Father.

You've a keen eye, the Father said. *I can see you're a man of taste. If I weren't a good Christian I'd drive a harder bargain, but the truth is that this room's to be converted, and we've no more need of it.*

Then the Father asking her, *Can you see yourself here, playing those fine, round notes all up to Heaven?* His hand in her hair, on her neck, then under her shirt because her father was gone then, off to the bank for the money, and the Father said he'd give her breakfast because it looked like she could use it, but all he did was tug her forward *why don't you and I just sit here a bit, on this nice, fine bench? What a shame it is to let it go.*

'Well, it's yours for the taking. I suppose you'll want to sell it,' said Fran.

Angie didn't know what the piano was worth. Maybe a thousand dollars. That would be a lovely windfall. She could get that leather coat she'd had her eye on, and that silver and turquoise bracelet she and Kevin saw at the mall. The rest she could bank for that rainy day that always came along so fast. Kevin, though, would want to put it up his nose. His cocaine habit used up all the money his father gave him. There was more money to be had, but his father had become difficult, and cut off his allowance.

'Good plan. Better to sell it here, though, don't you think?' Angie told Fran. That way Kevin wouldn't have to know a thing. *Listen, Babe, things didn't work out so well. That Fran, she's got things tied up tight. Must be how my old man wanted it, leaving it all to her. Figures, doesn't it?*

'Suit yourself, only I'm leaving first thing in the morning,' said Fran.

'Really, why?'

She spoke of a brother out in Santa Barbara, and needing a change of scene. It occurred to Angie that she could do with a few more days away from Kevin. They'd come to that hard point between lust and love, and spent more and more time on their bare mattress, a mattress she'd like some sheets for to cover the brown stains of her period, and the yellow stains of her sweat.

'I've got enough for one night at the motel, but after that I don't know,'said Angie and glanced at Fran, who stared firmly into space.

'I can stake you to a second night.'

'Oh, you're sweet! But don't you think it would be easier if I just stayed here? After you're gone, I mean. Don't like to be underfoot.'

Fran turned her leaky eyes on her. 'I'm sorry, Honey, you can't.'

Angie had visited last year with Boomer, Kevin's predecessor. When they left Fran found herself missing a silk scarf, a pair of gold earrings, and a fountain pen she'd won in a church raffle. Angie sometimes wore the earrings and scarf. The pen she'd never used. When her father called to report the loss, Angie blamed Boomer. She said he was a recovering heroin addict (he wasn't), and that he'd spent time in jail (he hadn't done that, either). Her father believed her. Obviously Fran didn't. Boomer, who knew nothing of the theft or the phone call, moved out several weeks later when he realized Angie had been helping herself to his wallet.

Fran offered to ship the piano down. Ann Arbor to Kansas City was a pricey distance, a fact Fran regretted with a lift of one eyebrow. Angie wasn't moved. There'd be no distance if Fran had stayed put. When Angie struck out on her own at seventeen, with no desire to finish high school, Fran pulled up stakes, and dragged her father up to her home town so they could float on the sale of her late husband's grocery store chain, forget the past, and begin again.

Angie wrote her new address on the back of a museum flyer Fran had on the coffee table by the whiskey. *The French Impressionists. February 4th - March 31st. Gauguin, Renoir, Cezanne, Van Gogh.* Angie couldn't imagine her father going to see that kind of nonsense, but then with Fran her father always thought he was better than he was.

'Well, then. I'll call a mover. They'll let you know when to expect it,' said Fran, and drained off her glass of whiskey.

She stood and tugged the jacket of her stylish black suit into place. Angie got up, too. She towered over Fran. Angie was five foot ten, skinny as a boy, with size-ten feet. She'd stuck out at the funeral with her torn jeans and red linen jacket. She looked down at the white roots running through Fran's dyed black hair and kissed her hard, right on the top of her head. Outside, the heels of her cowboy boots banged on the wide brick steps. Above her the sky was a tender blue, the yellow clouds a dream.

Fuck, she thought. It would have to be a beautiful day.

*

The piano was an upright, not a grand, and because a ramp had been built for a handicapped tenant some years before, the movers were able to get it inside Angie's apartment without loading it onto a dolly.

Angie shoved it across her apartment, around the coffee table which, she realized later, could have been pushed aside, to the wall by the kitchen. The wheels gouged the wood.

'Cool,' said Kevin when he came in. Then, 'Look what those morons did to the floor.'

'Yeah.'

'Better not lose my damage deposit.'

He smelled of cigarette smoke, which meant he'd been with Ramon again. Ramon was where Kevin got his coke. If he had any now it would be on loan, because Kevin's father was still being a jerk. Angie had met Ramon only once. He was so short she could have put her chin on his head. He worked as a car mechanic and promised to get Kevin hired on to do oil changes. Of course nothing had come of it.

Kevin went to the kitchen and made himself a peanut butter and jelly sandwich. Marta, his German Shepherd, clacked across the floor and sat politely in front of him. He offered Marta some sandwich, then pulled it back just as she opened her mouth to take it. After the fourth time, Angie said, 'Stop being such a mean fuck and give her some.' His blow sent her sideways into the kitchen counter. The blood tasted like metal, and made her suddenly remember falling on the school playground. Kevin stared at her. He was still chewing. The hand he'd hit her with had opened from its hardened fist and was poised in mid-air, fingers bent, like an old man's.

On the street, without her coat, she shivered. Her lip went on bleeding. She could feel it swelling. The Chinese restaurant smelled of hot grease as she passed. Bits of paper lifted in a gust of wind, swirled, then floated back to the sidewalk. At the corner a homeless woman sat on the steps of the church, her garbage bag below. She wore new track shoes with silver laces.

They looked at each other.

'Somebody got you good,' the woman said to Angie. 'Somebody with good aim.'

Angie stood with folded arms. Her lip throbbed. Behind a square glass pane on the wall by the door the message "I AM THE LIFE EVER AFTER" stood in white letters, advertising the sermon that coming Sunday.

'You go on in, clean yourself up,' the woman said. She drank from a tall plastic coffee cup, then looked at her wristwatch. Not homeless, Angie realized. Just sitting there.

'What you doing, Girl?' Angie asked.

'Name's Yolanda. Waiting on a guy. Coming to get a donation.'

'Of what?'

'What you think? Clothes. Food.'

'In a bag. You put it in bag.'

'You got something better?'

Angie went up the stairs. Inside was dark and smelled of dust and wood. The daylight leaked through the stained glass window. The ladies' room down the hall had a scent of bleach. Angie examined her lip in the small mirror over one of the two porcelain sinks. She felt her teeth. None was loose. On her way out a bulletin board with squares of bright paper caught her attention: *Babysitting, call Clair. Moving? call Jerome. Yardwork. Home Health Aide. Used van for sale. Wanted, upright piano for Church Basement/Nursery School.*

Angie took the long way home, down the street towards the record store and dry cleaners, then past the park where the children were warmly dressed. She kept walking until she was too cold to walk anymore, and then went home.

*

Kevin watched her across the candlelit table. The sky had given in to snow, and the power had gone out. Angie wore long underwear beneath a cotton skirt. On top she was naked but for a jean vest of Kevin's she'd grabbed in the bedroom. They'd had sex for hours. He'd dug inside her until she was as dry as dust.

'God, you have great tits,' he said.

129

'For a skinny girl.'

'For anyone.'

Kevin leaned back in his chair, his arms folded across his bare chest. Angie admired Kevin's arms, his shoulders, too. Sometimes she pressed her teeth there, and sucked up the salt on his skin.

'Know what I think?' asked Kevin. 'I think you're the kind of girl who can take a whole lot of a guy.'

'You'd know.'

'Maybe you can take some more.'

'Maybe.'

She sipped icy Vodka from the coffee cup. In four days her lip had healed a lot.

She'd been hit by men before. Not by Boomer, whose real name was Brad. The nickname had come from his mother, because he'd been such a loud baby. He wasn't loud when Angie met him. He never once raised his voice to her, except when he found out about the money. He called her a "cunt," which hurt more than she thought it would. Before Brad there was Toby, a bicycle messenger. He didn't hit her, though she'd hit him for cheating on her with their downstairs neighbor. Before Toby was Pat, and Pat had blackened her eye when she wouldn't get him another bottle of beer.

Kevin looked at the piano. He asked her again about selling it because now Ramon was pressing him for the two thousand he owed. Kevin's father was out. The last time Kevin called his father said, *It's time to face facts. All the money in the world's no use to you. And when are you going to get rid of that slut?* Angie didn't think that was the word his father would have used, and that Kevin had chosen it for effect.

'I'll get on it,' she said. She thought of the ad she'd seen, and of the piano returning to a church, going back where it came from, like ashes to ashes, and dust to dust. She laughed softly, then with a harder edge. Kevin went on watching her with his blue marble eyes.

*

130

Ramon sat at the far end. Angie waited for Noreen to get him, but it wasn't Noreen's station and Noreen knew it, so she let him sit.

He had the fidgets. One thick tattooed arm jiggled on the bar, one leather-clad boot danced on the bar rail.

'Hey,' said Angie, and put a clean square napkin down in front of him. 'Where's Kev?'

'Thought you could tell me.' He pushed his sunglasses to the top of his head.

'He said he had a job interview.'

'Not likely,' said Ramon.

'No, probably not.'

He asked for a Scotch and soda. She mixed it and brought it to him. He stirred it with the red plastic stick she'd dropped in.

'When you see him last?' he asked, looking at her tits. She saw herself in his eyes. The blonde dye she put in three months before had slid down and left a wide cut of black. Her pink tank top and the cold in the bar brought her nipples up like two ripe olives. Kevin's words, not hers. Angie had never eaten an olive in her life.

'This morning. Why?' she asked.

'He owes me money.'

She leaned over the bar. 'You'll get it.'

'I better.'

He drank his drink and she pulled back, towel over one shoulder, held by what he was about to say. And when he did she didn't have to agree. That's how it worked when you were there for the taking. Nothing had to be said.

*

'Ramon says he'll drop it to a grand and call it even,' said Kevin. Angie went on washing the dishes. In the dark window over the sink he stood reflected, hands on hips. He was a handsome man, with a fine square jaw, not at all like Ramon. Ramon's nose was broken, his skin was pocked, and his nails were filthy, but he trembled when he held her, even once cried out her name, and then talked of bad dreams, bad things remembered.

'That's good,' she said.

'I just don't get it, though. He was so hot for me to pay up.'

'I know.'

'He even went looking for me, down where you work.'

'I was there.'

He shifted his long, lean weight. She had to move fast, before he added it up. She turned off the water, and rubbed her wet fingers on her worn out jeans. The blood rushed in her ears, down her back, all the way to the soles of her feet. She'd crossed more than half the distance between them by the time he caught her by the shoulders. They made it all the way into the bedroom with her mouth pressed into his.

*

Kevin had a plan. He knew two things: where Ramon kept his money, and where he kept his coke. 'Cash in a coffee can, right there on the shelf. And the coke's sitting loose in an old box of laundry soap.' Ramon also had a gun which he kept in his bedside table drawer, and another one in the kitchen, inside an empty fruit bowl on the top of the refrigerator.

'Sounds risky,' said Angie.

'Only if I get busted, so I don't lift the coke. The cops won't ask about the money if they find it on me.'

'Still.'

'Come on, he's got at least a couple of grand. Plenty to go somewhere new. By the ocean, maybe.'

'He'll know you took it.'

'That's just it. There's this girl he used to live with, this Marcy something, and she's bad news, let me tell you. She comes in and helps herself to everything. He'll have to figure she took it. She's always after him for something. Major sleazeball. No surprise there, given the kind he likes.'

He dropped off and she was left to take one deep breath after another until she finally gave in to sleep.

*

In the rain she made her way down the block. The street was brown with dirt. Her skin was brown, too, and always had been. The big secret. Her father not her father. Her mother a woman who loved brown men so much she got knocked up by one, then left her husband for another.

The driver of a car honked because she was walking in the street. 'Fuck you!' she yelled.

She loved him anyway. The drunk who took her into bars.

The rain bent her face down, and when it lifted up there was Yolanda coming around the corner with a waste basket she must have emptied in the dumpster. Yolanda said, 'I remember you.' She had corn rows for hair, violet half moons for finger nails.

'You looking for a piano?' said Angie.

'Not me, the Father.'

Angie didn't like the sharp stare she was being given.

'All right, then. Don't be standing around in the wet,' Yolanda said.

She followed Angie inside, and set the waste basket on the floor. She went down the hall and knocked on one of the doors, then leaned her head inside. She closed the door and called back to Angie, 'He be right out.'

Yolanda went down the hall while Angie waited. The quiet was broken by the quick tapping of a radiator that slowed, stopped, and resumed like a sick heart not ready to quit.

He came out the door Yolanda had opened a moment before, a short, round man wearing black pants, a priest's collar, and a ratty grey sweater.

'I'm Father Mulvaney,' he said and extended his hand. Angie didn't take it. 'I understand you have a piano.'

'I can let you have it for fifteen hundred,' she said.

He nodded, rubbed his hands together, and stared into space just beyond her shoulder, as if he'd forgotten what he was going to say.

'Hm. Now, what kind of instrument is it?' he asked.

'Old and banged up.'

'An upright?'

'Uh, huh.'

'Out of tune, I suppose?'

'Probably.'

'Why are you getting rid of it?'

'What do you think?' Angie had put a few paces between her and the Father by then. He took her in with one long hard look.

'I think you could use a hot cup of tea, and a sandwich. I'm just about to have one, myself.'

Angie hadn't eaten breakfast that morning because she'd forgotten to get to the store the evening before. Sometimes she ate at work, if her boss left early. Last night he didn't, and she'd had two bags of M&M's for dinner.

'Nothing fancy. Just ham and cheese,' he said.

His office was small and full of books and papers. The radiator's paint peeled gray flakes that showed a darker gray underneath. She sat in the chair opposite his, separated by an old wooden desk. On a smaller table were a plate with several sandwiches, a teapot, and a number of cups, most of them chipped. Angie looked at the amount of food, wondering.

'Yolanda always finds a guest or two for me at the last minute. Saves the kitchen trouble by just having something made in advance,' said the Father.

'You must feed a lot of people,' she said.

'The mission down the street had to close its doors, and the economy hasn't picked up as much as we'd hoped.'

Angie finished her sandwich quickly, and the Father offered her another. She took it, but refused any tea.

She looked through the window into the courtyard where a man swept bits of paper into a dust pan. His arms reached beyond the too short sleeves of his shirt.

'What is it?' the Father asked.

'Why is that guy working in the rain?'

The Father looked through the window, too.

'Francis? Well, I expect he needed to get some fresh air. He's not overly fond of being indoors.'

Angie watched the man some more and wondered what it was like not to mind getting wet. When she turned away she found the Father leaning on his elbows, watching her.

'You pay cash, I'll drop the price a little,' she said.

His smile showed tiny uneven teeth. Above them his eyes were warm.

'I'm afraid I can only offer something very nominal.'

'Like, how much?'

'Can't really say, until I have a look at it.'

'Sure. You come by any evening. First floor apartment, end of the block going that way,' she said, tossing her head over her right shoulder.

Three days later Angie came home to find two bags of groceries by her door with a note *Sorry to have missed you. I'll come again. Father Mulvaney.* She took the bags inside and went through them. One had milk, eggs, butter, bread, frozen pizza, soup cans, spaghetti, even some coffee. In the other were flour, sugar, salt, a bunch of pretty fresh bananas, three oranges, and a can of peaches in heavy syrup.

'Who the fuck wants that shit?' said Kevin. 'Why doesn't he just cough up for the piano?'

'He will.'

'He better.'

That night Kevin was going to rip off Ramon. He'd say to meet him at the bar where Angie worked, and then she'd keep him there with a free drink or two. Angie's boss didn't let her give away drinks. She'd have to put her own money in the till. Kevin didn't think about that. He only had a twenty on him.

'I can make change,' she said.

'Forget it, will you?'

Ramon didn't come into the bar at all. Angie called her apartment once, twice. At two a.m. when her shift ended she went home. Marta hadn't been let out. Angie cleaned the dog shit off the floor, walked her around the block, breathed in icy air.

Angie's stomach was tight with hunger. Marta danced when the bowl of dog food descended from the heaven of Angie's human hand.

The phone rang when she was fast asleep.

'Babe, listen, I messed up.' He sounded funny. He was crying, she realized.

'What happened, Kev? Where are you?'

'Ramon was there. He tried to get tough.' It would have taken a lot more than a slap in the face to put Ramon down. Kevin would have had to finish it.

'Kev, what –'

'I can't believe it. I don't know what the hell happened.'

'Where are you?'

'Never mind.' He was quiet for a long time.

'Kevin,' she said.

'I have to go. Oh, and look in the piano. It's yours.' The line went dead.

She got to her feet, and padded along the floor. The living room was given over to moonlight from the curtainless window.

The piano lid took some lifting. The envelope inside contained one thousand dollars and the note, *You don't know anything.*

The night was clear, and the violet sky thrown with stars. *Take one down,* her father used to say. *That's what they're there for. Just reach up and take one.*

*

The morning light seeped over the window ledge, then flowed like clean water into the room. Marta lay warm beside her. Kevin could be anywhere by then, though if Angie guessed right he was at his father's in Indiana, the place he hated so much he described it with a fist to his head – the blue twinkling pool, the big white barn in the middle of fifteen rolling acres, the yellow forsythia hedge. His father would take him in, because money took care of its own. And he'd never get caught, because Ramon was just some drug dealer from Tijuana who'd had nightmares about the truck he crossed the border in, the sealed-up heat of it, the days without water.

Angie opened the kitchen door and let Marta into the little yard to pee. Marta squatted, then ran her nose through the dead winter yard until Angie called her back inside.

After she had dressed and sipped a reheated cup of yesterday's coffee, Angie took Kevin's expensive wool sweaters, heavy flannel shirts, and three pairs of good leather boots and put them in a green garbage bag. She put his books on the sidewalk in front of the house with a note, written on an old grocery sack, Free. His toothbrush she threw away. The toothpaste he'd used was hers. She wasn't surprised by the wetness of her eyes, or the tightness in her throat. Ramon had made her feel more at home than Kevin ever had.

Her neighbor, Joey, was sound asleep on a thrown out sofa two doors down. He wasn't homeless, but seemed to have trouble staying in his apartment at night. Angie nudged him with her foot, and he opened his gummy, red eyes.

'You want to make twenty bucks?' she asked.

He sat up, spat on the sidewalk, and scratched his head. His fingernails were filthy. 'For what?'

'Helping me roll a piano down the block.'

'You nuts?'

'You want the money, or not?'

Joey was several inches shorter than Angie, but strong. He had no trouble keeping the piano under control as it rolled back down the ramp. She took the other end, and kept it from veering off.

The day was overcast, the air calm. They pushed past parked cars, one with someone asleep in the back seat, another with a broken out windshield, and another up on blocks.

Every few minutes Joey stopped to clear his throat. When they reached the church Angie gave him his twenty.

'How come we brought it here?' he asked.

'That's my business. Now go on.'

The front door of the church was locked, and a side door, which gave on the alley between the church and the grocery store next to it was locked, too. There was a light on the second floor, and Angie threw a pebble at the window there, then another. The window lifted, and Father Mulvaney's head appeared in the open space.

'Who's making that racket?' he called down.

'It's here.'

'What is?'

Angie pointed to the piano, which was being closely examined by an old man pushing an empty shopping cart.

'So it is,' said the Father.

'It's yours. Free.'

'That's most generous of you.' The Father's face took on a look of worry as he watched her from above.

'Better get it inside before the weather changes,' she said.

'Miss – ' But Angie had gone around the corner by then, back to her apartment. She needed to give Marta another walk after breakfast, get the bag of Kevin's stuff to the thrift shop and take whatever they'd give her in return, then gather up her own things.

Then she'd find a pay phone, maybe by the airport, maybe by the stadium, some crowded random place where a trace wouldn't give her away. The call she gave the police would bring him in. He'd know it was her and one day, if he stopped hating her guts, he might realize that being taken wasn't the same as being bought.

Garden Story
By Nisha Woolfstein

Each time he pulled closed the heavy old curtains, it was necessary to hold aside the tumbling rows of plants, which lined the windowsill like toy jungles. The curtains would almost meet in the middle, leaving a chink of light showing the sunshine harsh and happy outside. The plants rested in the half-light of a low bulb, leaves hanging their sweet and damp scent over the high armchairs. At Christmas, timed exactly to the day, decorations would rival plants in overflowing, shimmering, thousand-leaved extravagance. Tinselled and candlelit, the room hid itself in forests of foils and folded papers, so that someone sitting in a hard backed wooden chair amongst it would not seem to be in the living room of a semi-detached bungalow at all, but rising out of the cluttered terrain of a different era.

But now it is summer, and the glimpse of light between the curtains is important. It teases, threatens too, because it is a link between the room inside, and the outside world of pavements and grass verges, the footsteps and shouts of children running past. A blackbird calls, ''do some more, do some more,'' amongst the ordered garden, between the pebble dashed wall, and the red gate marking a border as solid as that of a country.

The cotton dress, which she seemed to have worn for at least one whole summer, was probably pretty. It was the colour of apricots, and made from a fabric which seemed to ripple like a ribbon in the daylight. In the daylight too, it seemed somehow an adventurous thing to run the few streets barefoot, along the freshly mown verges and the hot summer tarmac. Thin white arms and legs that hadn't yet sprouted (though a year or so later, endless gangly appendages appeared like saplings;

overgrown), but they were still compact and self-contained, and she took them for granted.

In the early afternoons after school, sun streamed unashamedly through the glass porch, up the bare steps from the garden path, and across the yellowing lino squares of the kitchen. Sitting at the little kitchen table, he took quick hot sips of strong sweet tea, which disappeared between his lips and were swallowed in rapid succession, as a lizard might swallow a fly. She takes four sugars in her tea too, because she only drinks tea with him. Eyebrows raised with the sensation of heat, his face becomes all high cheekbones, leading to deep hollows where dark eyes sink amongst stretched, sun-leathered skin. One eye is sharp, just like a birds, the other is clouded over with the creamy fog of blindness; decomposing clouds of brown and white, like the mist on the shore of a sea.

In the mid afternoon, they go down the steps, and through the low glass porch, which smells slightly of moths and earth. The fresh air and yellow-green smells of the garden are startling. It is a relatively little garden. Bordered on both sides by gardens of the same proportions, precariously divided by fences (continuously rotting in the damp winters, only to be creosoted again next spring.) Over the fences to either side, patches of vegetables sit next to leaning apple trees, and the garden toys of children who have long left home flake rust like dandruff onto the lawns. But here, perfect rows of flowers stand nearly as tall as her, petals folding on vermilion and crimson. Lilac blending with yellow and exploding. The flower heads seem too big for their stems. He tells her how it was necessary to put little pellets around the flowerbeds, to stop the slugs from destroying the flowers, explaining that, once eaten, the pellet would swell inside the slug until it exploded. With snails it was easier just to crush them on the path. Years later, she seems to feel a disproportionate fondness for slugs and snails and slithering things.

'Listen. I told you about my father working at the manor house.'

She nods.

'Sweetheart, their gardens were the most wonderful. Lawns that had to be perfect. Perfect.'

'How perfect? Why…?'

'It took us all year working to make them smooth. Uniform. He was a very experienced gardener. Right. One day the family had a garden party.'

'Did you go?'

'I was the gardener. They were so rich that a great tent went up on the lawn. It was a sweltering day! Food. Cakes. Music. Dancing. The ladies all looking glamorous, all in the fashion, with their high-healed stiletto shoes,'

'What's a stiletto?'

'It's a shoe, very sharp. But do you know what happened the next day?

'The lawn was spoiled.'

'Ruined! Ruined!' He takes little scissors and dead-heads an over-ripe chrysanthemum. 'The ladies with their stilettos dancing and dancing. Full of tiny holes it was. Punctured all over, that perfect lawn of ours.'

She observes the carefully nipped flower, it looks like a shrunken head, with its blooming over. She wonders what a stiletto shoe might look like, and imagines a lawn full of beautiful women, who dance all day upon shards of glass.

The humid afternoon is such that, as they make their way from the kitchen through the narrow hallway, she can still smell the outside summertime even as they reach the far end of the hall and are faced with two closed doors, and another left just ajar. Through the half-opened door, Mr. Gander's living room is starkly lit by shocking sunlight.

'Wonderful day Sweetheart. Glorious!'

He stands back from the doorway to let her go through first, hugging himself tightly, like a boy, it seemed to Marta. He sees that her feet and her calves, her arms, are changing colour through the summer, not brown, but she's caught the sun. She feels solid there with furniture and irascible plants lit by the fierce day.

'Do you know what he said to me, Sweetheart…?'

'No, what?'

'He was a one in a million, Nell's husband.'

'What did he do?'

'He said to me, "I'm leaving her in your hands, George."'

'He trusted you…'

'He left her in my hands! My Nell!'

Lit by revealing sun and bereft of candle-light flicker, the altar today is looking as much like a neglected fireplace as ever it had, and Marta almost forgets the reason why they meet; feels almost as if she is simply visiting an old man on a sunny Saturday.

'Then you looked after Nell?'

'I loved her. It was the greatest love. We danced and danced all through the war.'

'All thanks to your eye!'

'Yes. Yes because of the eye, and because she had a husband in a million.'

He pulls the dusty curtains closed slowly while he talks; the process interrupted at each exclamation, where, firm-footed for his eighty-two years, he gesticulates sporadically with dark, weather-browned hands.

'All that people have now is the bedroom scene! It's awful. That isn't love Sweetheart. Worse than Animals!' Lighting a single candle beneath the Virgin on the way, George Gander sits finally in his Alter-side chair.

The music starts so unexpectedly as he recounts to her his wartime stories of illicit dances and ordained love. A few bars play before she hears and recognises it. Marta is surprised how it appeared from nowhere so gently. The music catches her like a light switch or a sharp sudden gust in imaginary sails, jarring her into familiar, open-horizoned, waters. Listening to the music now, she pictures it like golden rain falling, falling – and later at home she draws him a picture, where she is naked and the rain is golden. Now she cannot feel that this is a simple visit to an old man. Reasons collect on the horizon like rainwater, gathering and surging into a tidal wave. She tries to think about all the people in the world, all the people and the children and all of the animals (that are lovely and scary too, that have coats of sleek black or feathers red-turquoise, or golden lions manes or are giant like elephants – 'slow and kind' he says, and she thinks, yes, they are).

The weight of these thoughts crash around her as the music builds, but at the same time, when she hears this music it all becomes clear, and she can think about the stars going over one after another out and out and out and she doesn't cry. Marta often thinks it is something to make you cry, that there cannot be a wall around the edge of the universe, and more than that, that they expect her to understand. So often they watch her, waiting, and waiting, and it seems to make them happy when she tries to explain it all. But now, Rachmaninov makes it feel clear, that these stars are beautiful, and they make her cry inside without tears.

Marta feels fine now, she feels small. The music goes faster and faster like birds singing one after another and she knows she can do it - that she doesn't matter - that it doesn't matter if she can't have friends in her bedroom, or go running too fast along the road or ever kiss a boy like Alex, but only kiss Mr. Gander. And drifting, drifting so far. Far. She can see herself standing there, and Mr. Gander too, and she sees them small below her.

'I realised that Nell and I...' he speaks abruptly and pauses.

'You realised? What?'

'Like I told you. I told you. We knew each other, in the lotus pool. The love of long ago.'

'When?'

'Thousands of years ago Sweetheart! Thousands!'

'And now... you want to bring it back...'

'Yes! Now we can. We must. We must make it a reality.'

Marta's mind is drifting, now gusted out of its harbour by the music and how afternoons do change, change and change...thinking what if Mr. Gander was eighteen and not an old man, then I could say he was my boyfriend. He would have red hair like Alex and I could tell them at school and it wouldn't be a lie, because boyfriends can't be old men. But this is different because we are spirits. Her spirit is old, he says. They both have the colour red behind their eyes, and it is a colour which means power they told her. Only George and her had that colour, all the other ladies had other colours: blues or greens or yellow. She had red.

As he gets to his feet a bus chokes by outside the window, elephantine and growling, it briefly blocks the sunlight filtering through the curtains' ice-thin gap. When it has passed, Marta can see the dust in the fine edge of light which appears again. Dust like millions of tiny flies trapped between glass, but swarming and swarming through silver-grey light. The dust makes a wall which splits the room diagonally, so that Marta has to walk through it as she goes over to Mr. Gander, and the light

144

catches the edge of her eyes like a fishing line so that, as he kisses her, she cannot actually see him at all. Instead she notices, fleetingly, a ceramic duck hanging against the red of the wallpaper behind him. It is the middle duck of three which all fly perpetually over the nets of Chinese fishermen, in the corner above the record player. But as he presses his lips tightly against her lips, the duck too is blotted out because his hands grip her head as if it were a sea-encrusted anchor, and holds it there, clamped like a clam.

Every time he kisses her, his lips feel like the wet surface of a rock to Marta, not like lips at all, and his skin is always strange-smelling, like old rope. If he darts his tongue quickly it is a sudden scuttling crab. His nose protrudes at her like pincers. 'You won't be 'seventeen-and-never-been-kissed!'' He would sometimes say, laughing. She thought, how could anyone be seventeen-and-never-been-kissed, when she was only ten anyway... but all of this doesn't matter now because everything is so big, it seems to her it is enormous, and she has to do it, because she loves it, this earth. And all the people, the good ones, not the bad ones, of course.

She feels a short relief when he lets go of her head and puts his arms around her, she hugs him back and the three ducks above the record player come into focus again. The music itself has changed now, whirred from one groove of the record player to the next when they weren't looking, and Rachmaninov is nearly drawing to a close. Marta is glad that there are still a few bars of the music left playing, because it helps her to think that nothing matters. She will be able to do it because she has to. Then, if they killed her - Those in Opposition - it would have to be like that wouldn't it. Because she is the only one in the world that can make it all-right. The only one.

Learning to Float
By James Meredith

Anthony 'Tonto' Mullen stood at the edge of the high embankment and gazed down into the water below. The swing, which hung from the outstretched branches of the chestnut tree beside him, moved heavily in the wind; describing a lazy figure eight above the slow flowing river. The morning sun dappled the murky green water with dancing light and threw shards of silver onto a rusted pram, which lay half-submerged in the silt and slime of the riverbed. Tonto hawked up some phlegm from deep in his throat, rolled the soft oyster around his mouth, then spat towards the thick, brown rope of the swing, hoping to hit it. He missed and swore to himself.

He was waiting for his friend Willy Banks to turn up. They'd decided the night before to go on the beak from school. It was May, and they were supposed to be studying for their second year exams – Willy at Rathcoole and Tonto at Stella Maris – but Tonto was sick to death of sitting in a classroom wearing his coat all day, trying to keep himself warm because the windows had been smashed the night before.

It first happened during the summer break. The previous September, when the school bus pulled up on the first day of term, workmen were replacing the broken windows. Tonto walked past them on the way to Assembly as they manoeuvred ladders into place, sweeping away the shattered glass littering the ground beneath their feet, before climbing to join their workmates waiting in the classrooms up above.

The windows were broken regularly now. As fast as they were replaced they were smashed again. The school board had eventually seen sense and was in the process of having them boarded up while they tried to raise the money to have metal grills installed. Now when he got off the bus it looked to Tonto as if he was entering a derelict building.

It was because of the Hunger Strikes that things had gotten so bad. Bobby Sands was dead, and now every night on the news Tonto watched in fascinated horror as riots bloomed like tumours all over the country.

Bobby Sands had gone to his school, Tonto had been told. It was part of schoolyard legend. He'd lived in Rathcoole at the start of the troubles, and Bobby and the rest of his family had watched as his Da was dragged from his home by a screaming protestant mob and beaten half to death in front of them. Their house had been torched and they had to move out to West Belfast where it was safe. That's why he ended up joining the Ra, they said, and that's why he ended up dead. It was all the prods fault. That's what they said in the schoolyard.

But Tonto didn't blame the prods or hate them for anything. Willy was protestant, and so were half the ones he hung about with after school. They'd all grown up together. They were his mates.

Even at home they were talking about how bad things were getting. But his Ma and Da still sent Tonto to school.

'Aye, it's a shite time to be growin' up in Northern Ireland,' his Da had said to him. 'But when was it not?'

Tonto had had enough of the long, boring days in the classroom anyway, whether it had windows or not. He preferred to be outdoors kicking a football around or roaming through the glen, following its overgrown paths, exploring its dips and rises, and breathing in the wild smell of nature.

Willy was to meet Tonto beside the glen swing at nine. Tonto had brought some glue from his Da's shed. His Da was a builder who did some painting and decorating on the side, and the glue he used for his work was powerful stuff. Your head would fly off when you sniffed it.

Tonto wasn't worried about being caught mitching school by anyone. You hardly ever saw people in the glen during the day, except for other kids doing what they were doing, or the odd person out walking their dogs or taking a shortcut through to the shops on the Shore Road. If they did see anyone they could hide amongst the trees and spy on them, shout out to them, and call them names, laughing when the people stood looking about them, wondering where the abuse was coming from.

Tonto stepped away from the bank and climbed down towards the river, holding on to the exposed roots of the chestnut tree. He shrugged his Liverpool sports bag from his shoulder and yanked off his blue and yellow striped school tie, wrapping it loosely round his fist he unzipped the bag and slid the tie into it, beside the tin of glue. He hid the bag in a deep hollow at the base of the tree.

Down on the riverbank he was sheltered from the wind. He leaned up against the mound of hard earth that stretched up behind him for at least fifteen feet and gazed up at the branches high above his head. He unzipped the breast pocket of his bomber jacket and brought out a crumpled packet of John Player Black and a box of matches. He shook out a bent cigarette and straightened it between his fingers, then lit it and inhaled deeply, enjoying the dizzying rush of nicotine into his lungs and the anticipation of the day that lay ahead.

After he had smoked his cigarette Tonto moved to the edge of the river and got down on his hunkers. He flicked the butt across the expanse of water, aiming for the opposite bank. It cleared the river with inches to spare, bounced off an outcrop of rock, and then fell back into the slow moving water.

Then he saw Willy moving towards him through the clearing on the opposite side of the river. He had the collar of his school blazer turned up, and his blonde hair, teased with Brylcreem into a quiff, bounced in time to his long-legged stroll. Tonto had always found Willy's walk funny; the way he loped along on the balls of his feet, as if he was constantly testing the possibilities of flight.

Tonto stood up and waved across to Willy. 'Oi, ye tube,' he cried. 'What are ye doin' on that side?'

Willy walked to the edge of the bank. 'Did ye bring the glue, then?' he called over.

'Aye. All I could find was a big tin. Shoulder's near ripped off me carryin' it. Are ye comin' over?'

'Houl on,' Willy said. Stepping back from the edge of the water, he looked around for a rock. He found a good-sized one and hefted it in his hands. He moved back to the bank and threw the rock at the swing hanging in the middle of the river. The rock hit the rope right on the knot towards its base before splashing heavily into the water. The rope swung away from the force of the rock and then arced back towards Willy. He leaned out over the bank and grabbed hold of the rope with one hand, pulling it back towards him. He turned and climbed a few feet up the bank, twisted his body round, clenched the rope in both fists, and jumped. He swooped down low over the river, his shoes skimming the water, and then began to ascend. As he rose through the air he released his hands and landed with a whoop on the bank beside Tonto.

'Alright?'

'Aye. Where's yer bag?' Tonto asked.

'Didn't bring it.'

'What about yer lunch?'

'It's in me pocket. That all you ever think about, food?'

'Fags and glue, too,' Tonto said as he laughed.

*

Tonto and Willy decided to leave the glue for later. They took turns swinging back over to the other side of the bank. They followed the river up through the glen as far as the viaduct near Monkstown, watching from below as a train thundered by on its way into Belfast. They lay down in the long grass underneath the arches, where they were sheltered from the wind, and smoked a few cigarettes.

They didn't speak much; they just lay and enjoyed the quiet of the day, the soft gurgle of the river, and the freedom of not being in school.

They talked about the youth club disco the previous Friday night, and how Willy had got so pished that he fell over when he tried to do his rockabilly dance.

'That's what ye get for dancin' to that shite, anyhow,' Tonto told him. 'Ye shud get yer hair cut and get inta the ska.' Willy said he didn't want to be walking around looking like he'd just been to the nit doctor, which is what Tonto looked like. Tonto jumped on him and they wrestled until Tonto managed to get on top and pin Willy's arms to the ground with his knees. He sat astride Willy's chest and looked down at him as he struggled to free himself. Tonto pulled up a fistful of grass and threatened to rub it in Willy's face. The sweet scent of the grass perfumed the air and mingled with the heat from Willy's body. Tonto felt a liquid warmth rise up inside his belly as if someone was tickling him from within. Willy shouted 'give' and Tonto stood up. Red-faced, Willy began to fix his hair, checking that his quiff was still in place. 'You're gettin' fatter every day, Mullen,' he said looking up at him. 'One of these days you're gonna squash me.'

'That's not fat, that's muscle,' Tonto told him, turning away so that Willy wouldn't see his face. He walked to the edge of the river and leaned down to pick up a stone. He held it in his hand, rubbing his thumb over its water-smoothed edges, then wheeled around and threw it as far as he could in the direction of the current.

'Did ye ever think about buildin' a raft and goin' out on the river? Ye could start paddlin' away and then see where the current took ye,' Tonto asked.

'You'd end up in the middle of the Lough gettin' hit by one of the ferries headin' over the water,' Willy told him.

'It's just this book we're readin' at school, Huckleberry Finn. I was just thinkin' about it. I'd love to go on an adventure.'

'Aye, we're readin' it too,' Willy said, standing up and walking towards him. 'It's a good book. But sure you wouldn't need a raft. Ye get any bigger and ye'll be able to float all the way to Scotland.'

'Fuck off, ye lanky shite,' Tonto spat. 'C'mon, will we head back and do this glue, or what?'

'Don't ye want to have your lunch first?' Willy punched Tonto lightly on the arm and ran off laughing.

'Wait'll I catch ye, Banks,' Tonto shouted after him, and started running too.

*

The sun was high in the sky and the day had grown warm by the time they walked back. Tonto had taken off his bomber jacket and tied it around his waist; Willy had loosened his tie and opened the first two buttons on his shirt. They were making their way through the clearing to the glen swing, stopping every now and then to check the blue carryout bags that littered the glade, left behind by the fellas on the dole who lit a fire there most nights and stood around drinking. Sometimes the boys were so langered they left unopened tins of Kestrel or Harp behind them as they staggered off home.

Tonto came across a two-litre bottle of Merrydown, lifted it, and shook it gently.

'There's still some left in this, Willy. D'ye fancy a swig?'

'That could be piss or anythin' in there.'

'Only one way to find out.' Unscrewing the cap, Tonto brought his nose to the lip of the bottle, sniffed, shrugged, and took a tentative sip.

'It's a wee bit flat, but it's cider alright,' he said. 'Want some?' He held the bottle out to Willy.

'Yer alright. I'm not thirsty.'

'It's not for me thirst I'm drinkin' it,' Tonto said, tilting the bottle to his mouth and taking a long, deep slug.

'Fucksake! You'd drink anythin', wouldn't ye?'

'Long as it's booze,' Tonto replied, wiping his lips with the sleeve of his jumper then throwing the empty bottle off into the grass.

They walked to the end of the clearing. Tonto swung across the river, got his sandwiches out of his bag, and swung back across. They sat down on the bank and ate their lunch.

The glen swing had been there for as long as Tonto could remember. He didn't know who had attached the rope to the thick branch near the top of the tree, but whoever it was they hadn't been afraid of heights.

As they were smoking a cigarette Tommy Hur Hur came walking along the path, zipping up his trousers and trailing his black mongrel dog, Nobby, along behind him on a leash.

Tommy was a wee bit soft in the head. He was nearly forty years old and lived with his Ma in one of the bungalows at the bottom of Tonto's estate. He walked around Whiteabbey village with his dog all night, cadging fags or stopping to tell the kids that gathered on the street corners the latest stories he had heard about the ghosts that haunted the glen. Tonto thought he was alright. A bit smelly, but alright.

They called him Tommy Hur Hur because of his nervous laugh. When he talked he punctuated his speech with a "hur" or a "hur hur." He was dressed, as usual, in a shabby black suit, the knees of the trousers wrinkled and shiny with age. Unidentifiable stains marked the lapels of his jacket. Beneath his coat he wore a heavy green Aran jumper, and underneath that the twisted collar of a brown checked shirt poked out. On his back he had a brown leather satchel, like the ones the grammar school kids had. His large, red face was framed by a greasy black pudding bowl haircut that all the lads said his Ma cut for him. His mouth hung open, his dull grey eyes were ringed with the crust of sleep, and the stench of sour sweat clung to him like a cloud.

'Alright, Tommy!' Willy shouted over at him. 'Nobby takin' ye out for a walk again?'

Tommy walked over to them. 'Hur, alright lads. Any odds on yiz?'

'Sorry, Tommy,' Tonto said. 'We're both skint.'

'Giz a feg, then, hur.'

'What's it worth?' Willy asked him.

'Giz a feg an' I'll show yiz what I've got in me beg.'

'What is it?' Tonto asked.

'Hur, feg first, then I'll show yiz.'

Tonto brought out his cigarettes and gave him one.

Tommy Hur Hur tied Nobby's lead to the base of a tree, came back and sat down beside them on the bank. The dog began to snuffle around happily in the undergrowth.

'Giz a light,' Tommy asked, and Tonto passed him his lit cigarette.

'Show us then, Tommy,' Willy said.

Tommy slipped the satchel from his back and leaned in towards them conspiratorially. He undid the small brass buckles of the satchel, his fingers clumsy and stained brown with tobacco, and drew a magazine from the bag.

'Hur, it's a bluey,' he said with pride, passing it over to Tonto.

The magazine lolled like a concertina in his hands. It was bloated with damp and the front cover was missing. On the first page a blonde woman with bright red lips and heavy blue eye shadow sat perched at the end of a bed. The sun had bleached the picture, giving it the appearance of being overexposed. Mildew clung to the curve of the woman's breasts and a water stain scarred her smiling face.

'Where'd ye find it?' Willy asked.

'Up by the railway lines, hur.'

Willy leaned in close to Tonto and took the magazine from his hands. He began to turn the pages. He peeled them away carefully, reverently, as the glossy paper was stuck together at the edges. The next two pictures showed the woman with her breasts exposed, her dress bunched down around her hips.

'Hur, did ye ever see diddies like that before, lads?' Tommy Hur Hur asked, hunching in towards them. Willy continued to turn the pages until the woman was naked and lying on the bed with her legs spread wide apart.

'Fuck me,' cried Willy. 'Would ye look at that!' The three stared in silence.

The pictures made Tonto feel dirty, soiled, like the pages of the magazine. He thought the woman looked ugly lying there showing her big hairy fanny to the world, with a stupid smile on her made-up face and her tits held high in her hands. He thought about his Ma and what she would think if she knew he'd been looking at them. But he didn't want to stop looking.

Willy turned the page.

In the next photo two men had appeared in the doorway of the bedroom. One was blonde and the other was dark-haired. They wore leather jackets and flared jeans and were smiling at the woman lying on the bed.

'Hey, here come Starsky and Hutch,' Willy sniggered.

'Hur, Hur.'

When he saw the next photograph Tonto felt his chest tighten and his cheeks begin to bloom red. The two men were standing by the bed, their jeans hanging down by their knees, holding their erect penises in their fists as they watched the woman play with herself.

'Look at the size of yer man's knob,' Willy said. Tonto stared at the picture in the magazine. He was suddenly aware of the heat coming from the bodies that flanked him. His nose became sensitive to their odours; the smell of cigarette smoke, perfumed grass and the high, sour stench of Tommy Hur Hur invaded his lungs and spread throughout his body. His heart hung heavy like a stone in his chest.

Tonto felt spittle dapple his cheek and turned to look at Tommy Hur Hur, whose dull, pink tongue flicked in and out of his mouth and nervously licked at his lips.

'Hur, aye, that's some root on 'im, isn't it, Tonto? Hur. Hur.'

Tonto tore the magazine from Willy's hands and threw it violently at Tommy Hur Hur. 'Why don't ye fuck away off, now Tommy,' he cried. 'What are ye, a fruit or somethin'?'

Tommy backed off, his chin sliding down into his chest as he stared at the ground. 'I was only messin', Tonto. I'm no fruit,' he said quietly to the ground.

'Well, watch what you're sayin', if ye don't want a kickin'' Tonto told him, standing up and moving towards Tommy. Nobby the dog began to bark, baring his teeth and straining at his lead. 'And take that fuckin' mutt away with ye, or I'll kick its teeth down its throat.'

Willy stood up and spun Tonto around. 'Hey, calm down, fucksake. We're only havin' a laugh. Sure Tommy's harmless.'

'He tried to touch my dick, so he did,' Tonto told him. 'When we were luckin' at the pictures.'

Willy turned to Tommy. 'Did ye? Did ye Tommy?'

'N-n-n-no, ah ah didn't, Willy. Swear to God.'

Tonto watched as Willy walked up to Tommy Hur Hur, who turned his face away, readying himself for a blow. Willy leaned in close to him and said: 'Away on home to yer Ma, Tommy. Unless Tonto here wants to have a go.' Tommy raised his eyes and looked at Tonto imploringly.

'Aye, fuck away off, Tommy Hur Hur.'

Tommy stumbled over to Nobby, undid the leash around the tree, then turned and dragged the dog, still barking furiously, off up the path in the direction from which he'd come.

*

Tonto stood back from the high embankment holding the swing tightly in his hands. He ran parallel to the overhang for a few yards and then launched himself off into the air. He wrapped his legs tightly round the rope and settled his feet on the thick knot at its base. He swung low and then high in a great looping arc, his body cutting through the air in front of the trees on the other side of the river, close enough for him to reach out and touch them if he wanted to. Excitement rushed through him, filling his heart with a great joyful fear. It felt like the first time he'd gone on the Big Dipper at Portrush - only this was ten times better. The muscles in his thighs trembled as he squeezed the rope between them. He hung back his head and shouted into the sky.

The first circuit was the best. You couldn't swing any higher than that. You just went in smaller and smaller circles, lower and lower to the ground, until you had to jump off or end up in the river.

Willy was crouched at the base of the tree, pouring glue from the tin into two carryout bags that they'd plucked from the bushes. After Tommy Hur Hur left, Willy had picked up the magazine and put it in the inside pocket of his blazer. He'd turned to Tonto and told him that he had to watch his temper, that Tommy didn't mean any harm.

Tonto had told Willy that he was alright, to never worry, that Tommy was probably just overexcited and didn't realise whose leg he was touching. They had a cigarette, and then took turns swinging over to the other side of the bank to get the glue.

Tonto moved over and sat down beside Willy in the shadow of the tree. He took the carryout bag that was offered. It hung heavy in his hand like a bag full of coins. 'Christ, did ye put enough in d'ye think?' he asked. Willy just laughed and lowered his face to his bag, taking deep sharp breaths, his fingers kneading and squeezing the base. Tonto could smell the glue in the air all around them.

*

The sun was low in the sky, peeking through the intertwined branches and leaves of the chestnut trees, casting a golden glow onto the softly flowing river. Willy lay amongst the grass in the clearing. His clothes were soaking wet. He'd tried to swing across the river from the bottom bank and had fallen off the rope, landing in the water with a splash and a cry of delight. It served him right, thought Tonto. Willy had been hardly able to stand up straight, never mind use the swing.

Tonto lowered his glue bag and began to climb up the bank, holding on tightly to the roots of the tree. He was flying off his face. Somewhere in the depths of his head he could feel the beginnings of a headache, but right now he felt magic, he felt fandabeedozee.

The afternoon breeze caressed his face as he stood at the edge of the embankment looking down at Willy. He was great, was Willy. They'd be mates forever. And it didn't matter what happened, or what he thought about as he lay in his bed at night. They were friends, and that was all that mattered.

Tonto closed his eyes and watched lights dance upon the movie screen of his skull. He could feel the heat from the sun reaching inside of him, reaching inside and lifting him up. Suddenly everything made sense to him: the past, the present, and the future that he did not yet know, but would grasp firmly between his fists and make his own.

He opened his eyes to the golden afternoon. The thick, brown rope of the swing swayed lazily in the breeze. 'Hey, Willy! Watch this,' he shouted. Tonto flung his arms out in front of him like a swimmer on a high diving board, and with a great whooping cry he jumped for the rope.

Two Men in a Car
By Digby Beaumont

Where did you meet this woman? Mikey says.

Walter keeps staring straight ahead. In the Babylon Lounge, he tells him.

The two men are in a BMW saloon parked opposite the entrance to the underground car park of the Metropole Hotel in London's Paddington district. It's a little after 1.00am. Mikey is sitting behind the wheel. So, what happened? he asks. He likes a good story.

Walter lights a cigarette before he begins. It was last Friday night, he says. I got in there around eight thirty, I suppose. The place was empty, except for a group of three women sitting up at the bar. I ordered a drink and started to look at the evening paper when one of them came over to my booth.

Hi, she said. What are you reading?

She had the ugliest face. She was bulky, too. Wore a tank top — the kind with the midriff showing. Fat hung over her belt.

Gross, Mikey says, and he wrinkles his nose.

She noticed I had the paper open at the day's FTSE report. Asked me if I played the markets. I dabble, I told her.

So, how did you fare today? she said.

Walter draws on his cigarette. I liked that 'how did you fare', he says. It sounded quaint. Not so good, I told her. There was a big sell-off. Blood on the streets.

Sorry to hear that, she said. Why don't you let me buy you a drink?

Walter's mobile rings. He stops and takes the call. Jamal? he says. Yeah. We're all set. As he rings off, he looks at his watch. He'll be here in fifteen, he tells Mikey.

There's silence then Mikey says, So, this woman, she bought you the drink?

Walter rubs the back of his neck. Yeah, and we got talking. She could rabbit, that one. Said her name was Sheri and she worked in a call centre. Furniture supply company. Flat packs. Told me she was thirty, though she looked a lot older. I asked her if she was married.

No, she said, but I've come close more than once.

She was a big football fan. Arsenal supporter. Told me she went to her first game with her granddad when she was six. He stops talking and looks out at the car park entrance. The thing was, he says, once you got beyond the looks, she was quite a woman.

Yeah? Mikey says. There's doubt in his voice.

Yeah, Walter tells him, a character. He takes a last drag on his cigarette before stubbing it out in the ashtray. I asked her what had made her come over and talk to me. She was coy at first.

I'm embarrassed, she said. It was stupid of me.

Come on, I said. I'm intrigued. And you know what she told me? Said she'd done it for a bet, with her friends — the ones at the bar.

They bet me I couldn't have sex with you tonight, she said.

Fuck, Mikey says.

Walter turns to him. I asked her, How much was this bet?

Twenty pounds, she said, and she hid her face in her hands.

I laughed out loud.

Don't, she said. I feel terrible.

I said, Why? It's the funniest thing I've ever heard. I glanced over at her friends. They were grinning at us. When I turned back, she was blushing to her roots. But as I kept looking at her, I thought, Well, why not? So I squeezed her arm and said, Are we going to disappoint them? She gave me a wicked look.

Walter checks his watch. Five minutes, he says.

Mikey opens the glove compartment and removes a handgun, a Beretta 92. He checks the magazine and pulls back the slide. So, he says, and he grins, did she win the bet?

Walter lets out a breath. We went back to my place, he says. She stayed the night. It was amazing. The wildest sex.

Yeah? Mikey chuckles.

Yeah, but when I woke in the morning, she was gone. No note. No phone number. Nothing. I went back to the Babylon that night, but she wasn't there. Though I did meet one of the women I'd seen her with.

You two really hit it off last night? she said, and she gave me a little, knowing smile.

I told her it was okay, I knew all about the bet. Sheri told me, I said.

She pulled a face. What bet? she said.

That she couldn't get me into the sack, I said.

She laughed and said, Is that what she told you? No, there was no bet.

Then she asked if that was the woman's name — Sheri. I said, I thought you were friends?

No, she said, we'd never seen her before.

Shit, Mikey says.

Walter says nothing. There isn't time. A set of headlights have appeared at the end of the street. As they move closer, he can see they belong to a silver Land Rover Explorer. With a little screech of tyres it turns into the Metropole's underground car park. Walter nods to Mikey. That's our man, he says, and they get out of the car.

Not long after, two shots ring out. Seconds later Walter and Mikey re-appear and jump back into the BMW. Walter is clutching a large black briefcase.

While Mikey turns the key in the ignition and pulls away, Walter opens the case and starts checking through the sealed wads of banknotes it contains. When he's finished, he makes a call on his mobile. Jamal, he says. We've recovered your property. He won't be bothering you again.

When Walter rings off, he switches on the car radio. Music plays, and he settles back, lighting another cigarette before he turns to stare out at the shop fronts streaming past. Mikey checks in the rear-view mirror then his gaze returns to the road ahead. He's thinking about Sheri, can see her in his mind's eye.

I did it for a bet, she says. She's blushing to her roots.

Wonderland
By Sarah Young

Is all our Life, then, but a dream
Seen faintly in the golden gleam
Athwart Time's dark resistless stream?

Bowed to the earth with bitter woe
Or laughing at some raree-show,
We flutter idly to and fro.

Man's little Day in haste we spend,
And, from its merry noontide, send
No glance to meet the silent end.

-Lewis Carroll

I don't read Alice in Wonderland anymore. I don't because I can't. I can't because I hate it. I hate it because of my sister.

When I was three, my sister was born. I loved her immediately, but then I learned that she was a very permanent member of our family. At the age of four, I pushed her down the cellar stairs. I had watched in contempt as my infantile sibling learned to pedal her feet as she sat in her walker. Her joy grew as each slap of the pads of her feet on the floor caused the walker to slide in the direction of her choice. She was heading for the open door that lead from our kitchen to our cellar. My mind came up with only one solution.

She came out with only a scratch and my parents chalked it up to an accident. A few weeks after that, I bundled her up in her carriage, put on my rain galoshes, pushed her two miles down the road to the hospital, and tried to return her to the postnatal ward. They had a No Return policy. She came down with pneumonia and my parents couldn't find a good enough excuse to wrap their denial in.

When I was seven, I fell in love with Alice in Wonderland. Of course this meant that my sister also fell in love with Alice in Wonderland, and we would play it every day. My closet door had a full-length mirror attached to it that my Dad had nailed up years ago and was probably bought cheap from a Blue Light Special. It was trimmed with plastic that was a questionable shade of greenish-brown and crackled with age. That mirror was our looking glass, and we were the two Alices. Our mother even made us the tiny baby blue dresses with the white, lace-trimmed apron over top. We pushed our hair back with a black headband, rolled up our white stockings and strapped on our Mary Janes. Of the two of us, my sister always made the better Alice: her hair was the perfect shade of baby blonde, while mine, although still blonde, could only be crudely classified as dirty. Because of this, I'd constantly criticize her interpretation of the real Alice.

'Do you really think that's something Alice would do?' I questioned. Lyssa had added my Mom's enormous floppy hat, sunglasses, pearls, and ruby red heels to her costume.

'Sure, why not?' she shrugged.

'Alice isn't like that. She wouldn't wear all that junk.'

'Why, Lindy?' – frowny face.

'I told you. That's not what Alice would do.'

'Why?'

'Don't you listen?'

After we were dressed the part, we'd cross over into Wonderland by simply walking through the looking glass – or as everyone else saw it – opening the closet door. We'd spend hours sitting in the closet, lit by a single dim bulb, reading from Lewis Carroll's book or making up new adventures for the Alices to go on. Outside the closet was an extension of Wonderland, although the most exciting of Alice's adventures always happened on the other side of the looking glass. We believed in Wonderland like some people believe in miracles, in shooting stars, or in God. Although a part of me always knew that it was just a story, I always wanted it to be reality. My sister and I made it our reality. It was our obsession. My parents were just happy to see us finally getting along.

Funny thing about fantasy: sometimes in your mind it can become something so real, you feel as though if you just reach out, you can pet the Cheshire Cat, feel his matted fur between your fingers. Sometimes the characters feel so real that if you squeeze your eyes shut and open them real fast, you'll see them there. Just for a split second, before they flit away from your sight; along your eyelashes, and back into the corners of your mind. Sometimes you have intense conversations with Tweedledee and Tweedledum over the morality of the Walrus and the Carpenter, only to realize later that no one is there but you. Sometimes it reaches the point where you can't remember if that's your mother standing at the kitchen counter with the steak knife, or if it's the Queen of Hearts. You could have sworn you hear her mumbling 'Off with her head!' under her breath.

When I was nine, my sister began going to my elementary school. I was starting to grow out of the Alice phase, but she still liked it, so I would appease her after school, playing in Wonderland for hours on end. It wasn't exactly torture for me. When I was ten, my sister started hanging out with my friends and me during recess. At first I let her, but it wasn't long before she became the bothersome little sister I had loathed six years earlier. My friends didn't like her because they were too much older and too much cooler than her, and they made fun of me when my sister let the details of our after-school game slip out.

'Look,' I eventually told her, 'just go play with your friends in the first grade section.'

'They don't play Alice right,' she retorted.

'Play Alice?' My friends chuckled not-so-silently into the backs of their hands.

'Shut up, Lyssa. Go play with your own friends and leave me alone!'

She turned away from me and slowly walked toward the lowerclassman section of the playground, head down. I watched as she moved further and further away, becoming engulfed by the hyperactive first graders who swarmed the blacktop like ants fighting over a breadcrumb.

And then she disappeared.

*

When my sister failed to return to her classroom, her teacher immediately notified the principal and our building went under lockdown. The police arrived about thirty seconds after that. By one o'clock in the afternoon, police had staked out our school. My teacher managed to keep the class quiet until we saw the dark blue uniforms marching outside through the thick, warped glass. We erupted into discussion – what was going on? Were those cops? Why were they here? Did something bad happen? A half hour later there was a knock on our classroom door. Everyone screamed, even my teacher. An officer stepped into the room.

'I'm looking for a Lindsey Ullman?'

*

I asked my sister once as we sat in the closet, sipping out of invisible teacups, what she wanted to be when she grew up. She answered, 'Alice.'

'How can you be Alice?' I asked her.

'I'll just go through the looking glass into Wonderland and then I'll be Alice.'

'But you can't do that.'

'Why not?'

'Because you're not Alice of Wonderland, you're Alyssa of the Closet Behind the Mirror.'

'I can be anything I want.'

'Yeah?'

'Yeah.'

'Says who?'

'Mommy.'

*

'...Lindsey Ullman?'

The classroom collectively gasped. I stood up, confused.

'That's me.'

'Come with me, please, Lindsey.'

I looked at my teacher; she nodded. I knew what was happening, but at the same time I didn't. Did they know I yelled at my sister during recess? I thought about the time that Timmy Miller let his kindergarten buddy wander away from him. And how much trouble he got in after the kindergartener wandered back into the school building 45 panicky minutes after recess had ended, face scratched and bleeding, brush burn wounds on his tiny knobby knees. He told his teacher he had been playing in the woods. A playground monitor had been stationed near where the gravel trickled into the shady, wooded path ever since Timmy Miller's foul up.

'Am I in trouble?'

'No, sweetie, your parents are here to pick you up.'

'Lucky!' shouted Timmy Miller. My teacher shushed him.

The hall was desolate. We walked in silence side by side to the main office. It was a straight hallway and I could see my parents at the end of it – two shadowed, miniature people. I held up my index finger and thumb in a C shaped and looked through, framing them inside. Then I squished them.

I stood in front of my parents, looking up at their sagging faces.

'Where's Lyssa?'

*

A few days after Lyssa disappeared I stood in front of the looking glass, staring at my reflection. My parents said that no one knew where

Lyssa had gone, but I knew. Logic told me it was impossible, but instinct told me otherwise. She had gone through the looking glass.

The police were chasing any lead that they could find. After my parents realized that they had neglected to send me to school in over two weeks, they pulled me out permanently. Had I continued school, I would have been subject to hearing the rumors that swirled throughout the building. Everyone speculated about Lyssa's disappearance, my classmates, the teachers, and especially the secretaries. I would have learned that there was no more recess after my sister mysteriously vanished. I would have been the focal point for the attention deficit-spawned angst that came as a result of the lack of fresh air much needed after lunching on a PB and J with the crusts cut off.

My tutor came just weeks after I stopped going to school. He had a wide face and a mouth that held too many teeth. I'd ask him which equation I should use for math and he told me, 'One will give you the right answer and one will give you the wrong answer,' but wouldn't tell me which one to use. Then he'd grin with his mouth of too many teeth and his ears would perk up slightly. I'd think about how Lyssa would respond and come up with:

'It doesn't matter either way. We're all mad.'

He taught me for six more months until my parents let him go due to the fact that my IQ was slowly depleting with each obvious statement he made. My parents blamed it on what they called 'regression.' He seemed happy to leave. My next tutor was older, uglier, fatter. She slunk into the room like a giant caterpillar. Her breath reeked of smoke. I would work quicker on each assignment I was given in the hopes that she'd leave sooner. My grades went up, but my caterpillar tutor stayed. She must have had dementia because she'd always turn to me and ask, 'Why?' after nearly everything I said.

When I was 17 I ran into my first tutor. He still had the Cheshire Cat grin and didn't remember who I was until I jogged his memory with my sister's name. That's how most people identified me by then, with missing girl Lyssa Ullman. Guilty by association. He made the same O-shape with his mouth as everyone else did when the memory finally clicked. He then proceeded with the same line of questioning that everyone did, as if they all had a copy of the same script. My responses were as well-rehearsed as their lines were timed, and together they made for a beautiful skit.

*

When I told my parents at age ten about my looking glass theory, they stared at me vacantly at first.

'Looking glass?' my father asked.

My mother snapped out of it first, 'She means the mirror on her closet door, Greg. The one she and – she uses to play Alice in Wonderland.'

'Yes, and that's where she went,' I rationalized.

'Where?' my father was confused.

'Through the looking glass, she went through the looking glass. She wanted to be Alice and she went through the looking glass to be her. That's where Lyssa went!' My parents both cringed when I said my sister's name out loud.

From time to time I'd come into my room and see my father standing in front of the mirror. In the reflection I could see his eyes were bloodshot, vacant, nowhere close to reality. My mother never came in my room anymore – she'd only hold her breath and shut the door whenever she'd pass – so I would tuck myself into bed at night and listen to Lyssa playing in the closet. It was comforting knowing that she was content in Wonderland. I imagined her in her little baby blue dress with the laced-trimmed white apron, having tea with the Mad Hatter and March Hare and chasing after the White Rabbit.

The Hare: 'Have some wine.'

Lyssa: 'I don't see any wine.'

The Hare: 'There isn't any.'

The Hatter: 'Why is a raven like a writing-desk?'

Lyssa: 'I give up, what's the answer?'

The Hatter: 'I haven't the slightest idea.'

The Hare: 'Nor have I.'

Lyssa: 'This is the stupidest tea party I've been to in my whole life!'

My parents never told me when and where they had found Lyssa, so I had to make my own assumptions.

'If you saw the white rabbit, would you follow him down the rabbit-hole in the ground to Wonderland?' Lyssa asked.

'No,' I answered. 'Would you?'

'Yes. I would.'

'That's dumb.'

'Why?'

'Because, first of all, rabbits don't wear waistcoats or carry pocket watches–'

'This one does.'

'And two, rabbits can't talk.'

'This one can. He's from Wonderland. And I'd follow him.'

I came to the conclusion that Lyssa had spotted the white rabbit that day, lurking near the edge of the woods. Transfixed, she followed him into the woods, hoping he'd show her the portal to Wonderland. On the way she lost her black headband (which the police later retrieved) and in her haste to get to Wonderland, she let it go. It was a small sacrifice to pay for such a sacred place. I tried once, shortly after she had left, to see if I could find Wonderland in the woods, but my parents stopped me before I could get very far. A week after my attempt, a man with crazy white hair was arrested. I heard my parents talking about him late at night when they thought I was asleep. My mind came up with only one solution.

'How are your parents?'

'Divorced,' – the O-shaped mouth reappears for a moment.

'How are you?'

'Fine.'

'Did they ever find?...'

'Yes.'

'Where?'

'Under a tree in the woods.'

'Did they ever catch who did it?'

'Yes.'

'Who was it?'

'The Mad Hatter.'

The Silver Meseca
By Tom Gant

This will have to be the last time. It has to be. I promised.

Several brown birds bicker between themselves within the tree branches next to the petrol station and we start up again, continuing the drive coastward. It's Marcus' birthday, so we're on that same, familiar road once more.

A distant ocean comes into view as we arch over the hilltop and I pull over in a dusty lay-by. The view here is the best part of the trip and for a minute or two we trace the road below as it helter-skelters through olive tree groves to a few houses by the shore, beyond which an outlying haze of turquoise-blue promises a refreshing sea. The land below shudders in a watery and febrile heat; tarmac is glossy from the sultry conditions, and each corner is scarred by smudges of rubber from reckless local farm trucks used to haul fish up from the bay. The tyre tracks are faded, like aging tattoos. But then again, everything fades, one way or another.

'Well, here we are.' Marcus swigs a hasty mouthful of water from his bottle on the dash, 'Yet again.'

His first words since we got into the car, three hours ago. They're said with sarcasm. 'I guess we'd better make an appearance.'

'Yeah, guess so.'

I start the engine and ease us gently onto the road for the twentieth time.

Yes, the twentieth time in twenty years. I've counted.

*

Sammy lives away from town, way out on the headland. He told us it was to be closest to the water. Sammy couldn't bear to be away from water. Such feelings weren't unusual for an ex-sailor. After passing years on the ocean surrounded by waves each day and from every side, the desire for close proximity to large bodies of liquid isn't unnatural at all. Removing Sammy from the ocean would be the same as picking a flower and keeping it in a dry vase.

In recent years, he wouldn't recognise us at first and close the old wooden door with a curt nod and footsteps retreating back inside to some unknown occupation. Last year, he said people had stopped calling on him, so faces were becoming lost. Then again, I never remember anyone stopping by to see him anyway. Just Marcus and I each year, and his son, *twice a week,* Sammy would announce punching his index finger into his other palm as if to define the occasions. *He keeps me sane, boys.* Twenty years, same old door, same old visitors. We're into our forties now, and he still calls us *boys.* Nothing changes.

'Do you think he'll recognise us this time?'

'No idea,' Marcus answers, lighting a cigarette and planting a palm on the dash to steady himself as I turn another hairpin. 'I don't think he knew who we were last time, and we still ended up staying *three* fucking days.'

'Don't be like that.'

'Well I wouldn't be, but it seems like time to let things go. I mean, we've been visiting him long enough; we're a lot older now. Helen couldn't believe I was going away to spend my birthday with the old eccentric for yet another year.'

'Isn't she used to it by now?'

Silence. Marcus smokes.

'It's not just her,' he eventually mumbles, tossing the stub out the window, 'the bloody kids never get to see me on my birthday either.'

'I wouldn't know.'

'Look, we said last year was going to be the last.'

'We say that every year though. We've been good friends, Marcus, for the last thirty years and have been making this same trip for twenty. You know it'll never be the last. Not until…'

'Until he finally does the decent thing and decides to die?' Marcus cuts in swiftly, 'you *can* say it, mate! Don't look so upset either, he's not here!'

'It's not right to say it; you know that.'

'But I know we're both thinking it.'

'We owe him, Marcus. We owe him so much more than just an annual visit!'

I glare across the car and slam us out of a bend hard enough to renew the rubber scarring on the tarmac.

We continue unwinding the steep road to the ocean, curling between crisp dry olive groves with bare trees slotted deep into the yellow clay. Ramshackle huts patched together from sheets of corrugated iron and wooden fence posts appear at random intervals in the fields. Bone-thin animals - goats - stand in the shade of one such shelter and stare idly as we pass. Then just as I remember it, right when a foreign gnawing begins at the very back of the throat, the arid gnawing of dehydration, that's when the sweet blue ocean swells into view. Marcus decides to pick himself up from his slump and bellows, nay, *whoops*, like a man of twenty years ago. We drive the final stretch with his head out of the window, whoop-whooping to the blistering sky and goats and barren little houses. Only this time, I can't help feeling a hint of bitterness about him, as if he's playing out the satire of his past self.

He wasn't comfortable with coming again; it took a lot to persuade him, another promise of a final time. Marcus has settled now. It's become clear over the last few visits all remnants of youthful adventure have been drained from him. Twenty years ago we hitched down the winding valley on the back of an open-top Cherokee, music spewing forth into the countryside, a polluting echo right down the valley. Now, we're pulling his Chrysler down the road with air conditioning humming in the background. Our stomachs have grown, trousers ridden higher - aged. But then again, it's not just age, and it's not just Helen and his children either. He feels guilt. The familiar aching guilt we have all felt over one thing or another. His guilt for Sammy, I can sense it. We both do. We owe him so much; Marcus just needs reminding, that's all.

As we drift past the first few houses in town he cranes his neck forwards, searching. After a couple more buildings pass, we turn the corner and he sticks his head from the car window and shouts again, this time with a strong, genuine pleasure.

'Hey! I *knew*. I just *knew* it would be here!' He chimes with excitement, jerking back inside and clutching my shoulder like a child, 'I *knew* it! Pull over, pull over!'

He gestures to the roadside and I ease us to a stop alongside a large arch forming what used to be a gateway. The arch doesn't lead anywhere, just a ragged steel frame fronting a rubble pile of bricks and charred timber. Marcus leaves the car and skips a few feet from it, turning back to grin mercilessly.

'I *told* you! The Silver Meseca is still standing! Jesus Christ. This thing will outlive *everything* in this world. It hasn't changed in the slightest. Hey! Get a picture of me underneath it, will you?'

I sigh. Another event we repeat each year.

On top of the steel frame, draped throughout the full length of the arch, are row after row of dusky white bones, curling over and over again into a gentle semicircle. They're the ribs of some giant fish, caught years ago. I shudder to think now, how long since. Sammy told us about it, the moonfish. At one end, a large bleached skull droops downwards to a hanging jaw which looks as though it would swing if someone pushed it. Out here in the blazing heat, the skeleton fish is hung to bake on the top of the arch, left bare to turn white and desiccant beneath the blazing sun. It seems a sickening cruelty. A dreadful opposite, a horrific opposite! Like a bird being forced to crawl through wet earth or an animal pushed to walk over molten rock. Between each of the large ribs, other fish skeletons are draped dead and hopeless, mock flesh to the bigger fish.

'We must have a dozen, maybe two dozen pictures of it already!' I say through the open window. I've left the engine running. I can't bear to be close to it.

'Oh come on. You still hate the thing, after all this time?'

'It's eerie, that's all. I don't like it. It shouldn't *be* there, so out of place. Let's just get going.'

'I want a picture. We came all this bloody way just to see the old man; the *Silver Meseca* here could be pretty much the only good thing to come out of this whole trip.'

'With that attitude it will be.' I answer, still speaking from inside the car.

'What'd you mean by that?'

'I mean you could at least make the most of it, we should be here and you know it. We're doing the right thing, and besides, it's only for a couple of days.'

Marcus sighs and turns his back to me, saluting the twisted monument in a comic-ceremonious manner, his short legs stamping to attention. He stays a few seconds before sulking back to the car and into the passenger seat.

'We'll have to come back at night, when it *glows*,' he says finally, bargaining, 'you can't say it doesn't look impressive then, all silver in the moonlight.'

'I suppose.' I mutter in reply and hope he forgets the idea.

'It must have been caught under a full moon and hung up there on the same night, all silver scales and shining. Hence *Meseca* – sort of a bastardized word for moon isn't it?'

'Yeah, but it's still all so strange.'

'Well, you *know* Sammy.'

*

Marcus smokes and I knock on the warped wood door again. Still no answer.

'Maybe he's...' he taps his cigarette and after meeting my gaze, drifts off awkwardly, '...*you* know?'

'What?' I play dumb.

'*Dead,*' he answers in a hushed voice. My face obviously gives displeasure away because he hastily continues. 'There'd be no way to know, that's all I meant. We don't contact him; we *can't* contact him. Only visit.'

I tell him I'll go look around the back. His notions aren't something I want to listen to, not after coming all this way. We'd have found out somehow, Sammy would've got someone to tell us, a letter from a lawyer or a phone call. Or, or his son. Of course, his son would have contacted us if anything had happened; he knew we visit, after all.

Sure enough, as soon as I turn the corner I see a figure in the distance, out on the headland squatting down close to the waves. The outline of a beige suit can be seen and soft reflection from the thin grey hair, just the same as ever. I beckon Marcus from the porch and he joins me with an apologetic shrug.

'Sammy!' I yell across the headland, 'Sammy!'

The figure doesn't respond, so I start walking out towards him when Marcus' hand falls on my arm. It's a gentle grip, soft enough to stop me to listen.

'Look, mate, we don't have to do this again.' His voice is lower now, and more sincere. He is suddenly the Marcus who joined me in the past, only more grey around the edges. Edges that have swollen outwards, fatter, older, exhausted.

'I know. It's just...' I trail off and look out to the silhouette against the waves as he continues.

'It was a long time ago, he *knows* we're thankful and all that. But we have lives now. Twenty years have passed, *twenty years!*' Marcus is still clutching my arm; he knows I don't want to listen to this. 'We've changed since then, grown up. You've gone bald, we're both fat and middle aged, I've gotten married – my children, wife, they don't understand all this, it's...'

'Well I haven't got those last things,' I snap back, wrenching my arm from his grasp, 'and this means a lot to me. We wouldn't have even *had* the last twenty years if it weren't for Sammy.'

'It may appear that way at first, but he's not a good person, Aaron, you know that.'

My name in Marcus' voice. It forces our eyes to meet, forces us to recall.

Drowning.

Marcus and I. Drowning out there in the looming black mass of ocean, late one night in summer, thrashing against the waves desperately attempting to reach our rental boat from which we were tipped, like soldiers from a box. Waves lashing over and upon us. The wooden craft was later found in pieces, scattered all up the coast and gathered up by local farmers to build fences. Our bodies, flailing back and forth. Thrown by nothing back against itself, over and over. To drown in a storm is to die through repetition. The same motion over and over, fighting against them until your body becomes too tired to repeat the loop anymore, much too tired. Instead, it just gives in and down you sink into icy wash, like being immersed by the coldest of cold sweats. Now, round the back of the house I see myself twenty years younger in the reflection of Marcus' eyes.

And I'm still drowning.

'He saved us though.' I hear myself mutter. Marcus is miles away. He came out of it worse off than I did, lying in bed for weeks. *Fever* the doctor had said. *Shock* or *trauma* - they weren't invented back then.

'That doesn't make him good,' Marcus answers, finally drifting back to the present. 'Sammy's bitter; a twisted old soul and you know that as well as I do.'

I say nothing. Just stare at the figure by the shore - a clean suited old man who dragged the two youngsters, *boys*, us, from death's door.

'Let's just get it over with,' Marcus says, shaking his head and walking out to meet our saviour.

'Jame? Jame?' He doesn't turn around.

'No, no, Sammy, it's Marcus.'

'And Aaron.'

'I hear your footsteps, son!'

We're almost upon him, and as though he has been biding time during our approach, he turns and I draw breath, reminded once again of the same crooked grin as the one wet with seawater, the one which dragged me from the ocean and flopped my beaten body, deflated, out onto a ship's deck. That crooked and uncanny grin with rolled back cheeks and buckled teeth crammed tight. So tight they seem to creak against each other underneath the bloody outlines of clownish lips. Greying patches of skin show between cheeks of otherwise lunar pallor with blushes of a sickly yellow about the mouth, always twisting into the same crescent simper. His skin almost matches the pale beige suit he wears, well cut and fine fitted around his figure.

I always remember, years back, studying Freud in college, and his essay on the uncanny: *Terror, derived from something familiar, but just not quite right,* our tutor had described it as. Sammy is an old man, one expected him to look old and worn, but at the same time there's something strange and uncomfortable about his appearance. He always seems clean and fresh cut, opposing his surroundings completely. If there was a simple way to describe Sammy, it would be as the personification of uncanny.

Time hasn't altered him, though. He's always seemed old to us, a festering stoop in stature, but hidden well by nimble command of the aged limbs. Though the eyes, the eyes have remained constant and unforgettable. How could they be anything else? Those small dark orbs set firm within Sammy's skull have been something to which time's effect falls futile. Something unique and at first disturbing. Since birth (so we've been told by locals in town) the pigment facets in Sammy's iris began to leak, spilling gradually into the white of his eyes until they too turned a dark brown. His eyes have the appearance of huge black pupils; two still ink wells. Never turning to look or focus, but at the same time, *always* turning to look or focus.

He stares our way for a full minute before recognition dawns and each of our hands is clasped in his own and we heave him up from the rocks. I forget how small Sammy is as he dashes his suit down.

'Boys! Is it that time of year already?' He wheezes and struggles to catch breath after standing and speaking so soon after each other.

'It is,' Marcus answers, still clasped in the old hand, 'how are you, Sammy?'

'Ah, you know me. Just fine, just fine.' His eyes sparkle slightly.

'Good, good,' Marcus continues, eying me nervously, 'we were wondering if you'd like to get some dinner or something?'

'Starved. I'd *love* to get some,' he growls, clearing his throat and repeating in a low tone. '*Staaarved.*'

The vowels are drawled out in a way to makes me shudder. They always used to. As if noticing me for the first time, Sammy turns and grates out my name with the vowels left trembling in the air.

'*Aaroun,* m'boy, and how *are you*?'

'Fine thanks, Sammy. It's good to see you again. Maybe we can all go to the restaurant in town?'

*

Our first visit after the accident was more like a one off. Marcus met Helen the same year, and I was dating Laura back then, so we all went as a four. A kind of pilgrimage. Most of the time was spent reminiscing and paying gratitude to Sammy through cooking meals and continuous praise and thanks from our girls. He would sit back and smoke a pipe, pleased by the attention. His dark eyes would drift between us through the grey haze, though it was hard to tell where he looked exactly. Knowing Sammy, it was probably at the girls. For those few days we felt truly lucky to be alive, each hour a gift, an extra that only Marcus and I were benefiting from. However, there was always a suggestion of something being wrong, even then.

The morning after the accident, I awoke in a hotel room with a doctor administering to Marcus who lay in the next bed to me, deathly pale. I knew it was a hotel because a Monet print hung on the wall in front of me. There was no hospital twenty years ago. A woman in the hotel looked after us for weeks, bustling into the room daily with home cooked fish soup and fetching a doctor whenever Marcus was bad.

'How are you this afternoon?' She asked me on our first day as I sat beside Marcus' bed watching him grow paler.

'I'm ok,' I answered, indicating to Marcus, 'just worried about my friend, you know?'

'Ah, you were both very lucky. He's swallowed a lot of seawater, but he'll survive.'

'I know, thank God for the fisherman.'

'Oh,' she started, 'that's no fisherman. *He's* no fisherman, and certainly has nothing to do with God. Yes, yes…you were both very lucky indeed.'

'I'll have to thank him…once we're both better.'

Marcus groaned and I remember feeling so relieved I could have kissed the bustling old woman right on the spot.

'*Marcus*,' I gestured, but she took my arm and placed a finger on her lips.

'Let him sleep, he's not through it yet,' she eased me away and back towards my bed. Then her voice lowered. 'I also suggest you stay away from him.'

'Who? Marcus?' I answered defiantly.

'No. Silly! Not Marcus, dear. Sammy: the man who saved you. As I said, you were very lucky indeed. Try get some sleep.'

And with that, she was gone. It took Marcus a full two weeks before he could leave his bed, frail as a child, to join me in a trip out to the headland.

'Oh, it's no problem, *boy*,' Sammy chirped from a chair by his porch door. 'It's no problem at all.'

He was smoking a thin cigar, ruminating, and beamed his appreciation at our visit, making us even more uncomfortable with his eyes.

'We were - er - wondering if you'd like to come out for a drink with us in town?'

'*Where* in town?' A suspicion furrows his brow.

'There's only one bar,' I laugh, trying to break his sudden change of mood, 'so I guess we'll probably be going there.'

'No,' Sammy says, standing up and pacing a little towards the ocean. 'No. We'll stay in here. You boys bring some whiskey from the store and we'll drink it out on these rocks.' Then, turning to see our confused faces, he added, 'The sunset is beautiful from this headline. That's what we'll do. Trust me, *boys*.'

So we went back to Sammy's that evening, and most evenings afterwards. We always took a bottle of whiskey, and on occasions our host would fetch a bottle of local schnapps from inside and we'd get drunk out on the rocks on the headland. They were sombre evenings, on reflection, but pleasant nonetheless. We ignored Sammy's appearance, his blackened and empty eyes. He was always quiet, speaking only of himself and the visits from Jame, his son.

'Goddamn it! Aaron, man, why do we have to keep going back? We've told the old man we're thankful.' Marcus moaned as we entered the store to pick up drink for our umpteenth visit. It was a similar sound to the one he first made back in the hotel room during his recovery.

'We're leaving in, what? Two days? We can spare the old man some time,' I snap back and ask the shopkeeper for a bottle, 'you of all people should be grateful. You nearly died, after all.'

'I guess,' he hands me over some money to pay for the whiskey, 'but all we do is sit in silence, maybe talk about *sea voyages*. It's just so bloody boring. We should be out in town picking up girls, not sat inside with some old bloke.'

'Well...' I saw his point, but didn't want to. Still, I was young, and time with Sammy was wearing thin. 'Let's get Sammy into town tonight then, we'll insist.'

'Excellent,' Marcus brightened. 'Besides, the old fella is probably sick of us by now anyway.'

He wouldn't come. We insisted over and over again until in the end we left him the bottle and took off for town by ourselves. He gazed after us with sadness in those big black eyes. The day after, I awoke and felt guilty as hell for not visiting him; he had saved our lives and delivered us back to the safety of the hotel. We were in his debt, a lonely old man who we'd abandoned.

As we came downstairs to the lobby, the old woman who had been so kind in nursing Marcus back to health was standing pale and sweating by the reception desk.

'You two!' she hissed upon seeing us, pointing a fat finger in our direction, 'you pack up and get out right now. I shouldn't ha - I shouldn't have let you stay here, not after...'

With that, she disappeared into the back of the hotel and left us standing at the foot of the stairs.

'Jeez, what's all that about?'

'No idea, man, I guess we'd better pack our stuff though.'

'Marcus?'

'Yeah?'

'Do you, do you think we should see Sammy before we leave?'

'Christ's sake! I knew you were going to ask that, even before you spoke,' he answered, exasperated. 'I'm sure he'll be fine without us.'

We left the hotel later, only to be met on the steps by utter commotion. The hotel lady and her husband – a pale man who read the bible religiously and hated us for wearing our hair long – were both standing in the middle of the path; he appeared to be steadying her. At first, it seemed they were simply taking air, until we drew alongside them and saw the pool of blood which had formed across the entrance to the hotel garden, underneath the large metal archway. A fish, maybe six feet in length had been slotted onto the steel spikes at the very top of the structure.

'Fucking Christ,' Marcus muttered, gazing upwards.

'Get out!' The hotel woman's husband turned on us. 'Get the hell out of here and never, never come back! You've cursed this place. Damn you, damn you both!'

That night, as we waited for a train back at the mainland, we heard a radio report of the fire; an inferno which blew across the whole town, scorching the wooden house frames within hours, destroying everything. The emergency services said it started in the hotel kitchen and due to the dry summer and strong breeze from the ocean, spread too fast to ever be controlled. Most of the town was destroyed.

*

'Restaurant's closed,' Sammy purrs as we walk back towards his house.

'Since when?' says Marcus. 'I could have sworn we drove past it on the way in?'

'You won't have, not anymore.'

'Say, the *Silver Meseca* is still hung up there on the archway.'

'Of course it is,' Sammy bristles, 'nothing will get it down.'

I notice he says *it* and not fish. Twenty years have changed it from something recognisable into something completely different.

'I still can't believe it survived the fire,' Marcus continues, 'something so frail could have gone straight up in the blaze.'

He should have stopped. We know Sammy doesn't talk about the Meseca. I had brought it up with him when we visited as a foursome, asking Sammy if he knew how it had got there. He'd turned defensive and told me he didn't know, how it had nothing to do with him, and we should never talk about it again. I think that was the first occasion Sammy properly scared me. Now, Marcus continues, pushing it and Sammy is starting to scare me again.

'Mind you, bone might not burn that easily after all.'

Sammy is silent, just staring at Marcus and I realise we've stopped in between the headland and his house in a tense triangle, each one facing the other.

'Let's go Marcus.' I say, tugging his sleeve. I knew this would happen. 'Let's get some food for tonight. We'll eat on the rocks.'

'Oh yes, my meal,' Sammy spits, 'don't forget, will you? Don't forget my *meal, boys*. Don't forget me again, *boys.*'

I drag Marcus away and Sammy remains, looking at us like an injured animal through those glossy black eyes.

*

'You shouldn't have talked about the Meseca like that, you know how he feels about it.'

'What? Because the sick old bastard hung it up there?'

'You can't prove it. I asked him, remember?'

'Yeah, and what was the response? A load of mumbled gibberish and a spooky look in the eye. You can't trust Sammy, Aaron. As I said, he's not a good person.'

'Shut it, Marcus! Every time we come, every year. You have the same bullshit ideas about him. Fine, he's a little eccentric, granted, but he saved your damned life. And you can't even give the man a break.'

'Fuck off.' He breathes and doubles pace away from me.

We shop in silence, leaving the empty store with armfuls of thick rolls of rye bread, beef tomatoes, garlic, paprika, and two bottles of whiskey. I pay the bill this time; I'm not as poor as I used to be.

'Sorry man,' Marcus says as we leave the store. I stop on the edge of the pavement and turn towards him. He lights a cigarette, 'I guess I just have a hard time dealing with this stuff. I always have, you know that. When we came with Helen I could barely sleep, I have nightmares,

Aaron, horrible dreams about this place. Us two out in that boat, into the water, drowning.'

He takes several long drags and shakes his head. 'I just want to forget it. I always have wanted to, ever since the first trip back to his house when you insisted on thanking him. I wanted to forget it when we got back home, when we found jobs and settled. I actually went a full year once, the one when Susie was born, where I didn't think about it at all. But now, now the dreams are back, and, I don't know if I can do it anymore.'

I honestly hadn't thought of it like this before. Of course, I'd thought about it, the accident, unavoidably. But for me, just seeing Sammy, regardless of *who* he was, or is, seemed like repayment. As though the time given to me, was given by him, and is being earned through visits, superficial gratitude. Sammy, he controls me from thousands of miles away. Laid in bed at home, I realise now that I think of him, late at night-time. I thank him, over and over again. Getting on the tube in the morning to go off to work, I bow my head and give a silent thanks to Sammy in his house on the headland. Each day is a gift from him. I just don't want to be ungrateful.

Explaining this to Marcus is too difficult. There aren't words for such a feeling. *Debt* or *guilt* would both be words he'd use, but they're wrong. If forced to label it, self-requisite gratitude is what I feel towards Sammy. I'm sure he doesn't think I owe him anything, but imposing such sentiment on myself, well, it helps.

We start walking along the shoreline through the town. The place has become deserted over the years. Windows boarded and sealed from the outside by rusty nails and rotting wood. Crumbling render scatters the deserted street. The occasional roof tile lies shattered in the gutter. I realise we are walking through what has effectively become a ghost town. Fire damage still marks a lot of the buildings, and the ones that have been rebuilt are those boarded up from the outside. I shudder as we pass the hotel, keeping my eyes on the cluttered pathway so as not to see it: The Silver Meseca, the silver moonfish, sprawled on the archway, the only thing to remain.

'I swear that thing gets bigger,' Marcus says as we pass by. 'There are smaller fish padding it out. The damned thing is nearly the same size it was when it was alive.'

Oh, yes, the pool of blood on the pathway as we stood alongside the hotel owners was from a *live* fish. It twitched mercilessly. Every now and then, it shuddered in spasms of silent agony. There must be no pain greater than pain endured in silence. As the bible-reading husband shooed us down the stairs and underneath the impaled corpse I remember the tail suffering violently in our direction.

'You ok, Aaron?'

I'm doubling over with my hands on my knees at the very memory of it.

'Fine,' I grimace, pulling myself up, *'just fine.'*

Marcus pats me on the back and we continue.

'Well, he doesn't look to be outside so I guess we're going to be dining in the house.'

'Surely not? We've never been past the front door before?' I question, a strange tingle passing through my body.

Marcus knocks, waits, tries the door. It opens and he calls inside.

'Sammy! We're back!'

'Sammy!' I join in, trying to ignore the strange fragrance in the air.

'Crazy old bastard,' Marcus mutters under his breath as I follow him through a narrow corridor, 'which door d'you wanna try?'

'Not fussed,' I answer, pushing the nearest one. 'Might as well start somewhere.'

As the door swings aside, a vision comes to me far worse than any I've seen. Worse than drowning or the dead fish. Far worse than those. Ivory; hundreds and hundreds of bleached sticks form a collage of osseous matter, plastered across the walls and ceiling of the room. They spiral between each other to form hideous chalky imprints, shapes resembling nothing at all, just uniform patterns, repeating over and over.

'Oh...my God.' Marcus gives a cry that is no more than a breath. 'What is this?'

Reaching out, my friend lets his fingertips roll across the ghastly decorations and I see him shudder, recoil.

'Let's get out of here,' he says, turning in horror at the realisation of what he has touched. 'These are *bones*, Aaron, just like the Meseca!'

A look of madness captures his face, and in panic, he dashes forward and flings open a door on the opposite wall, hurtling through it. I follow close behind, calling out with a head spinning.

And there he is. Sammy, standing in the centre of an empty room, caught off-guard by the sudden entry he is pivoted to the spot right in the middle of another collage; a different pattern from the previous room; still formed from intricate moulding and fitting of blanched cuts of bone. I realise the strange fragrance is sweet, the smell of decay.

He turns, eyes blazing darker than I had ever seen before.

'GET OUT!' he screams, arms lifting above his head. 'YOU SHOULDN'T BE HERE!'

He rushes at Marcus with such speed it takes him off guard, sending him crashing to the ground. Turning to me, Sammy squares up, his body clenched into a wild stance of attack. I realise this is impossible, a man who must be well over eighty could not stand a chance, though I see Marcus groaning on the floor and take my assailant by the arm as he rushes forward, twisting it behind his back.

'Take it easy, Sammy.' I bellow, moving him towards the door, outside and away from the horror. 'Come on Marcus! Let's get out.'

Sammy's struggling, heaving against my grip, kicking at my shins frantically and all the time I bellow for him to calm down. Then I lose it and wrench his arm a little too far. A sickening crunch and Sammy screams in agony, breaking loose and striking me across the face over and over.

'It was me! Me! I caught the Meseca from somewhere!' Sammy shrieks, thrusting an arm towards the ocean. 'Somewhere out there! And - and I dragged it all the way into town under moonlight, and I draped the fleshy thing right on top of the archway spikes and left it to ROT!'

The breeze slows and the night flushes warm, if only for a moment, before Sammy starts over again in the rasping voice, grating away at our ears, constant.

'And when you left me, for town, for those people who have no faith in me, who run from the man with dark eyes, well, I paid another visit to the Meseca, oh yes I did.'

I feel sick. Closing my eyes, I see them both. Sammy standing under it, the crooked grin illuminated and glowing as the hideous carcass droops lifeless above him, out of place, altered. A fish drawn from its life in the ocean, just as Sammy had been. A reunion of the uncanny, the slightly affected. Solitude.

I know what Sammy is going to say next. Marcus has always hinted, all these years, but I refused to let him say it. I refused. I didn't want to believe it was true.

'And I burned it all to the ground.' He laughs.

God! Not once had I heard him laugh until now and a feeling of disgust replaces the one of nausea for it is the laugh of a madman.

'I *knew* it!' Marcus starts, turning to me as if for confirmation. I stare back dumbfounded. 'Didn't I say? He's a bad person, Aaron.'

'You said he isn't a good person, Marcus, there's a big difference you know.'

He ignores me and starts to pace up and down in the middle of the path, one hand forming a finger, which he taps into the air.

'Oh, oh, this is bad,' he says, over and over. 'This is bad, very bad. I *knew* you had something to do with it. This is why we could never talk about the damned thing. And the fire! Well I wouldn't put it past you, but even I'm surprised. People *died* in that thing you know, dozens of people!'

Sammy breathes out audibly, a long guttural sigh of satisfaction, which stops Marcus in his tracks. I can't believe this is happening.

'Liar, Sammy! You're a damned liar!' I yell, blinking back tears.

'What do you mean, *Aaroun*?'

'You promised me Sammy. You - you fucking well promised me.' I storm across to the other side of the path and bend in two, hands on knees again. I feel betrayed and sick to the stomach. The man to whom I thought I owed everything, for whom I lost hours of sleep over, *worshipped.* He deserved nothing. 'You said it had nothing to do with you. All these years, every time, you feigned innocence.'

'You're a *murderer!*' Marcus yells hysterically. 'All this time and you've betrayed us. Tricked us.'

'What do you mean?'

Marcus looks straight at him, like staring at the sun, his eyes start to flush dark, undertaking some strange fever, heat from the past is being dredged to the surface. I feel it too, a maddening betrayal, wild and unleashed from deep within the self.

'Does your son know any of this?' I ask, trying to lower my voice.

'What do you mean?' he repeats dumbly, a wet grin forming on his face. He raises both eyebrows and lets out another long guttural laugh.

'What *son*?'

Marcus is bleeding and wipes a red stain from his forehead onto his sleeve. The sight of his own blood sends him staggering backwards in disbelief. I look into his eyes, right into them, and see myself in the darkness once again, still drowning.

'Bleeding?' Sammy asks, cackling madly.

*

Sammy's house is alight and Marcus is whooping again, jumping up and down ahead of a backdrop of flames.

'Yaaaaaa! Freedom! Yaaaaaa!'

The place burns slowly. A suitably dark, dull red throbbing of heat. Bones must be burning inside, cracking, splintering. Their marrow melting down between each one, running silver blood down the walls and onto the floor. I see the Meseca turn its cold white head towards me from somewhere in town and shakes. No, it *rattles*. It rattles itself. Once so graceful, it now rattles a path through existence because it has been places where it's not supposed to have been. That's what happens when things are taken from their natural habitat: they warp and disfigure into something…something *uncanny*. Now, it gasps in the air, the dry night air, so cold beneath the moonlight.

I don't know where Sammy is anymore, but I'm right next to the water. I feel the cold breeze against my skin, lapping softly. I hear wet thumps and feel something slump through my fingers and through the rocks, back out into the ocean.

What the Birds Say
By Lauren Farnsworth

Alex had been in bed for ten minutes. The bedroom was so humid he sweltered beneath the covers as the numbing weight of sleep began to pull his limbs under. The heat of Moira's body beside him pressed against his skin; he felt it like a touch, heard her breath, the pauses in the spaces between where her heartbeats might be. When she shifted, his eyelids twitched awake. The mattress bounced as she sat up, piled pillows against the headboard and burrowed back into them. She grew still again, her breathing long and deep. Alex fell back under.

When Moira murmured softly, Alex felt his fingertips tingle, where consciousness had begun to creep back. He wondered if it had been a dream.

'Did you say something?' he asked.

'That bird. I said, can you hear it?'

'What? What bird?'

'That bird out there, can you hear it?'

'No.'

Lying on his back, he inclined his head towards her. Moira sat straight-backed on the edge of the bed, her pillows bunched as indistinct shapes against her.

'Listen,' she said, and they did, to the thick silence of the room, swelling further in the moments between their breathing. Moira's quiet, drawn out breath. Alex's coarse and laboured huffs through his mouth.

'Can you hear it?'

'No.'

She became quiet again and Alex let his eyes close.

'There! Again! Did you hear it?'

He turned his face from her, away from the window where the darkness was heavier and more complete.

'Well where is it then?' he mumbled.

'Well I can't see it.'

'So how'd you know it's there?'

''Cause I can hear it. Clear as day, I can.'

'No birds out at night anyhow.'

'So much you know,' she said a little louder. 'I can hear it clear as day.'

The mattress rocked as Moira swung her legs back onto the bed. She pulled the covers up, away from him, leaving his arm exposed.

She sighed shortly. 'You need your ears cleaning out, that's what you need.'

Although she couldn't see, Alex nodded. He nestled his head under the sheets at the base of his pillows where the cool cotton rested on his forehead and the hollow hushed away the sound, but with a sudden movement, Moira's elbow dug into him.

'Did you hear what I said?'

Alex grunted into the covers.

'Al, I said did you hear me?'

'Yes I hear you,' he said, 'now hear me. I'm trying to get some sleep here.'

'Well I can't. Not with that bird singing out there, I can't.'

'There ain't no birds out there. You're hearing things is all. Now hush. I'm up at five.'

He listened to the seconds ticking out on the clock, mingling with the rhythm of his breathing and the beat of a small pulse on his temple. A night symphony. A lullaby. A minute passed and he felt almost blessed.

'You think they're saying anything?'

Alex deliberately deepened his breaths, snoring a little, though he did not usually.

'Alex, I said do you think they're saying anything?'

His eyes snapped open. The room had begun to grow so uncomfortably hot that he itched with it.

'For Christ's sake, who? Who's saying something?' He shoved himself up on an elbow, and with his fist curled into a hefty ball, he thumped at the centre of his pillow.

'The birds!' Moira cried softly. 'The birds, do you think they talk to each other?'

'What are you on about? Birds can't talk!'

'I think they do. I don't what they'd say, but I think they do. What do you think they say?'

'How the hell should I know?'

'But what do you think?'

'Flying? I don't know.'

The bed jerked as Moira sat up again. Then came the rustle of her nightgown, the sounds of her smoothing back her hair. 'That's stupid,' she said. 'That's like humans getting together and talking about walking.'

Alex burrowed so deeply the bed appeared to have swallowed him. It was even hotter here, he began to sweat, but it was also quieter.

'That's stupid,' she said again. 'I don't know what they're talking about but it sure ain't flying.'

'If you're so interested in talking why don't you go out there and join the conversation? Leave me some peace and quiet.'

'He's not having a conversation, Al. There's only one. You can't have a conversation with yourself.' She drew in several hesitant breaths, seeming to want to add to it. 'Having a conversation with yourself,' she murmured eventually. 'That's just crazy.'

'You seem to be doing a fine job of it.'

Apparently just satisfied with him saying something, Moira leant towards him. She laid a hot hand on his back, pressed into the soft flesh beneath his shoulder blade.

'So ... what do you think they say?'

Alex clenched into his pillow. 'God knows at this time of the night. Bad manners, if you ask me, talking and talking at this hour.'

The palm of her hand came down to swat him on the shoulder.

'Some people like to talk at night,' she told him in a fierce whisper. 'Some people find it quite appealing.'

'Well birds ain't people, are they?'

'No,' she said quickly. 'No, I know that, but some people like it is all. That's all I'm saying.'

'And some people have to be up at five.'

'Fine. Go to sleep. Just go to sleep then. That's fine.'

Alex felt another jiggle and the absence of Moira's weight for a moment. He heard the curtain rings rattle on the rail as they were drawn, the creak of the window being opened. Moira lay back down.

Gentle tides of night breeze drifted in, dancing on Alex's uncovered skin, leaving goose bumps behind as footprints. The sultry bedroom air began to melt.

Outside a shrill bird made himself known by trilling out a high, chaotic melody, and then finding no reply he began again.

'Goddamn it, Moira, close that window. That chirping's driving me nuts.'

Alex rolled over to see Moira's eyes closed, her lashes fanned half-moons on her cheeks.

'Moira. Moira, I said close that window. Moira!'

But whether or not she heard him, she still did not stir and kept her eyes shut.

The Dictionary of Loneliness
By Jessica Phippen

I once knew a man whose world sat in his dictionary. The pages contained whole continents, the Northern Lights and mountain ranges; pens and pencils; furniture; assorted haberdashery; boxes, both empty and full; picture frames; lives; the passing of time, past, present, future and the spaces in between; ands; ifs; nouns; love. Adverbs huddled in the shadows of the binding, adjectives slipped between the cracks in the cover, verbs transcended the space between one page and the previous or the next. Nouns hung from the tips of t's, the ends of y's and j's, and fell into pits of the u's, or were trapped in the mighty and inescapable o. They slithered down z's, and reclined in the gracious c. And this is where Leo Bernstein lived. He climbed up the w's and mounted himself on the m's, one foot on each bend.

I met Leo when he was living with his son and daughter-in-law. He'd left his apartment in the Meatpacking district when he had suffered a cardiac arrest. The doctors had suggested that he move into a nursing home. Leo's son, in a fit of nobility, had immediately declared that his father should move in with him and his family. With his wife out of town, he felt he was able to make such a decision, but when she had returned to find Leo in the guest room, she resumed full control - sending her husband into fits of disgruntled uselessness. Leo's trips in and out of the apartment were regulated by his daughter-in-law, and she was also the one who shepherded him to his bi-monthly check-ups.

'What's your daughter-in-law like?' I asked him during the first few hours of our tentative friendship.

'She is a practical girl,' he shrugged.

'Meaning that...?'

Leo gawked at me. 'Meaning that she is "clever at doing and making things."' He thumbed through the worn copy of *The Oxford Paperback Dictionary* that he carried in his pocket. He found the definition he sought and held it out to me. I glanced at the page, and discovered that he had written his daughter-in-law's name, Hannah, in the margin beside the definition of the word "practical". He had also scrawled the name beside the words "preach", and his son's name, Benjamin, by the word "pout".

Leopold had grown up surrounded by books. He even went so far as to say that his house didn't have walls, but rather, large piles of books that divided a single space. He said that he had read *The Divine Comedy* three times before he turned twelve. Granted, he didn't understand it until he was at least sixteen, but a great achievement nonetheless. His parents decided that young Leo would also be brought up in an extremely secular house. Thus, Leo claimed to have a kind of wondrous inattention to religious affinity or race, paired with an unparalleled understanding of the world. This was all due to his parents and his upbringing, so he said.

However, this supposed understanding of his was somewhat marred by his complete absorption of the dictionary, or the dictionary's complete absorption of him. Over the course of his life, Leopold Bernstein had come to inhabit it, completely and utterly, so that his mind became a sea of definitions and etymologies.

So this was Leo's state when I met him. But I struggled to find the trigger of Leo's obsession, the beginning of his love affair with the Oxford English Dictionary. And when I attempted to draw this information out of Leo, over café mochas and croissants in the dim, mahogany lighting of the West Village Café, he would only remove himself into the crypt of his mind. The deadened mass of knowledge that was his world. Sadly, I could never manage to lure him back out again, because the truth was that Leopold didn't like the world in which I lived, the world that he presumably used to live in. So, whenever either was truly mentioned, he would seek out the world in which everything was carefully, thoroughly, easily defined and understood.

When I first met Leo, I was working in an independent bookshop in Chelsea, called "Bookends". Fresh from graduate school, I had moved into an apartment about the size of a closet with two other girls that I knew from school. One, Amy, was at Law school at NYU and the other, Melinda, was working at Power House books in Brooklyn. The older couple who owned the bookshop had known Leo for years, and hired him just two years before to work there, but I didn't meet him until one month into my job, in the sweltering heat of a New York summer.

I was huddled in the back of the store, in the poetry section, arranging and stacking books. I had a copy of Yeats' *Collected Works* in my hand when I heard Leo's voice behind me for the very first time.

'Excuse me, but I was wondering there was a copy Ted Hughes' Birthday Letters buried somewhere in there, preferably not the Faber edition.'

I turned around and looked at the man who had spoken to me. He was tall, lean with age, his face furrowed with wrinkles, but his eyes were bright green and alive. He had a few wisps of grey hair on his head and wore a pair of thin, square glasses that were perched precariously on his nose. He gazed down at me sweetly, his eyes vibrant, yet gentle.

'I think we have an Everyman edition, let me check,' I turned around and searched the shelves behind me. 'Yep, here it is,' I pulled it out of the stack and handed it over to the man behind me. He held his hands out for it, they shook a little, and he took it tenderly, balancing it in his hands. 'Thank you very much.'

'Of course, is there anything else I can do for you?' I asked him politely.

'Have you read this?' he asked, holding up the book of poetry.

'Yes, several times.'

'Which is your favourite poem?'

I thought for a moment before answering 'The Owl'.

' "I saw my world again through your eyes, as I would see it again through your children's eyes", he recited. 'Lovely poem. I like 'Remission' myself.' He seemed lost for a moment, as if he were reciting the poem to himself. I watched him closely, trying to remember how the poem went. The silence stretched out until it became somewhat awkward, so I went back to my work as he stood there with the copy of *Birthday Letters* in his hand.

Finally, at the point when I had almost forgotten that he was there, he spoke again. 'Can I help you with that?' I turned around, surprised and a little confused to look at him.

'Excuse me?' I murmured.

'Can I help you with that?' he pointed towards the stacks of books. 'Elaine and Tom usually have me stacking books because I'm useless with the cash register. Far beyond my technological capabilities, I'm afraid.'

'You work here?'

'Yes, I've been working here for over a year now.' He gazed at me intently before gasping. 'You must be Elizabeth.' He held out his hand to me.

'Yes,' I took it, slightly bewildered.

'I'm Leopold Bernstein,' he introduced himself.

'Oh yes!' I said, smiling, 'I've heard about you.'

Over the next week, Leo and I became friends. He explained that he had been gone for a month due to some medical issues. In the hospital, all kinds of tests were performed on him while they tried to figure out exactly what was wrong with his heart. This is when he told me about his son Benjamin, his daughter-in-law, and his granddaughter, Isabel.

'What about your wife?' I asked him casually, as I took a sip of my latte.

He lowered his eyes and his shoulders seemed to tense. 'She's not around.'

'I'm so sorry,' I whispered, 'when did she die?'

He shrugged and said nothing. He wouldn't look at me.

Die: 1. to stop living

After Leo and I had been steadily getting to know each other for three months, he invited me back to his apartment for dinner with his family. Curiosity is one of my weaknesses, so I accepted and I must admit that I looked forward to the day somewhat ravenously, preying on my calendar greedily and with much anticipation. Ever since Leo had first mentioned his daughter-in-law, I had been interested in meeting her myself. Our conversations carried through a wide variety of topics - World War II, Bush, comma splices - he hated these -, Shakespeare. But he always managed to avoid the topic of his daughter-in-law. He spoke of his son freely, his granddaughter, even more so. But hardly ever mentioned Hannah.

When the night finally came, I made my way over to Leo's apartment and, a few minutes late, arrived outside the door. I noticed the heavy silence in the building, the moody lighting, the smell of freshly-laundered clothing. I knocked on the door, after seeing the "Broken" sign on the doorbell. I heard faint voices and then a moment later the door was open. Standing there was, I assumed, Leo's son Benjamin. We stared at each other for an agonizing moment, until he finally recognised the impolite silence and hastily greeted me.

'Hello.'

'Hi.'

A pause.

'You must be Benjamin.'

'Yep.'

Another pause.

'I'm Elizabeth.'

'Benjamin!' a woman appeared at his side. She had a pinched mouth, wide green eyes and a long straight nose. Her hair was dark brown and straight, and she stood with an air of confidence that I found almost overwhelming. 'Why don't you invite our guest in?'

He obeyed her instantly, opening the door wide enough for me to enter. As I stepped into the apartment I had to shut my eyes for a moment. It was unusually bright - perhaps in comparison with the rest of the building - that it blinded me for a moment. Benjamin offered to take my coat. He took it and hung it on the coat stand then went over to join his wife, who was inspecting me with those eyes of hers. A pause.

'I haven't even introduced myself! How incredibly careless of me!' she said with great degree of civility. 'I'm Hannah Roeke, Benjamin's wife.'

'It's a pleasure to meet you,' I took the hand she held out to me and allowed it to be vigorously shaken up and down.

I heard feet on the hardwood floors and saw Leo come into sight around the corner. He beamed, seeming almost relieved to see me, as if I was providing him some vital service. I grinned less brilliantly back at him and drew Hannah's attention away from me and to her father-in-law. 'Leopold, your guest has arrived.'

'I noticed,' he answered. He moved to stand beside Benjamin, and all three of them turned their varying gazes upon me.

'Thank-you very much for inviting me over for dinner,' I said politely and somewhat anxiously.

'After everything you've done for Leo, it was the least we could do,' Hannah replied. Her voice betrayed an attempt at warmth as well as its underlying iciness. I felt more chastised than thanked.

We moved into the living room, where I was invited to take a seat. I sat between Leo and his son with Hannah in an armchair across from us. What followed was a barrage of questions, from Hannah, with several interjections from Leo, solely about the varying definitions of this word or that, or its Greek or Latin roots. I was equally amazed by Leo's knowledge as I was by his daughter-in-law's miraculous gift for making one as uncomfortable as possible. My only respite came when Hannah and Benjamin's daughter - Isabel - entered and asked to hear a bedtime story. Hannah agreed, sent a rough smile my way, and left with her daughter in tow. I heard Benjamin let out a sustained breath, as if he had been holding it all throughout the interview. He seemed to relax beside me and I took this as an opportunity to begin a conversation with him when he was perhaps, at his most approachable.

'How old is your daughter?' I asked.

'She'll be six a week from tomorrow,' Benjamin replied, his voice soft, almost a whisper.

'Is she your only child?' I continued.

'Yes, Hannah only wanted one,' he nodded, then hastily added, 'I'm going to go check on dinner.' He got up, glanced at both of us hurriedly and rushed out of the room.

'He's a very good cook,' Leo smiled, staring wistfully at the seat his son had occupied.

'I don't doubt it,' I replied, nodding.

Leo looked over at me, his lips stretched into a smile that seemed to express such understanding. And then his face contorted. His left arm was quivering. His hand flew to his chest, and he fell back against the couch.

'Leo?' I said, jumping to my feet and placing my hand on his shoulder. 'Benjamin!' I cried. The note of urgency in my voice must have aroused some dormant energy in Benjamin, and he came running into the living room almost instantly after I had called for him.

'Call 911,' he said. His voice was so calm, so composed, that I could do nothing but gape at him for a moment. When he urged me again, I moved towards the phone; it seemed an eternity before someone answered. Leopold Bernstein. Eighty-two. Hannah re-enters, her daughter in her arms. Cardiac arrest. Leo is lying back on the couch, his hand still pressed to his chest. 12th between 5th and 6th. Apartment 6A. His son hovers above him, moving with a purpose. Hurry.

2. to lose force or activity

Benjamin and I waited. Hannah was dropping Isabel off with a friend, while we endured the torture of the unknown. The silence stretched out before us, one of profound deepness, in which each of us was hardly aware of the others existence, so greatly were we entrenched in our own thoughts, our own worries and wonders about life and death. I wanted so badly for there to be a definition for this, this unknowing, this darkness, this absence, but I could hardly find the words.

'Mr. Bernstein?' a doctor stepped into the waiting room, a clipboard underneath his arm, gazing at Benjamin curiously.

'Yes,' Benjamin and I both got to our feet.

'Is this your wife?' he asked, glancing at me.

'No, she's a friend of my father's,' Benjamin replied.

'All right,' the doctor nodded. 'Your father is stable, but there were some complications…we're running a few tests. I don't want to make any inferences, but…' he paused, glancing once again at me.

'Can we see him?' I interrupted.

'Yes, of course, come with me.'

I allowed Benjamin and the doctor to walk ahead, giving them some privacy to discuss Leo's condition. For some reason I didn't want to know what was wrong with him, I didn't want any of that horrible knowledge. I just wanted to see him.

We entered Leo's room, the blinds were pulled down, the lights off, all except a lamp beside his bed that veiled the room in a soft artificial glow. Half of Leo's face was lit up, highlighting all the wrinkles, all the marks of age that seemed so much more prominent now than they ever had before. The doctor excused himself, leaving Benjamin and I alone with Leo. Neither of us moved, for fear of disturbing the other, of intruding upon the other's privacy.

'I'll leave you alone with him,' I said to Benjamin as I left the room. For a moment I stood in the hallway, frozen, and I seemed to be floating in the air, above all the doctors and nurses. And I could see into all the rooms - see all the patients- , all the people waiting, just as Benjamin and I had been. But for some reason I couldn't see Leo.

3. to wish very much

Several hours later, Benjamin and Hannah went to check on Isabel, and I was left alone with Leo. He had been awake for about an hour, and scarcely any words had passed between us. He lay in his bed, suddenly seeming fragile and so incredibly sad; skin sagging over his thin arms, hair tousled, wrinkles deepened so that they seemed to be great crevices that stretched across his face. But his eyes, those bruised eyes, were filled with such serenity. I felt that this was the moment to ask him a question which I had been curious about for some time.

'Leo,' I said, so quietly that I was almost certain he didn't hear me, 'where's Benjamin's mother?' There was a long pause, until finally his lips moved, having difficulty forming the words, perhaps because of his ailing strength, or perhaps because these were the words that he most feared.

'She left.'

I reached over and picked up his copy of *The Oxford Paperback Dictionary* and flipped through the pages until I reached L. There I found that the verb "to leave" had been scratched out, with such severe pen strokes that the ink had sunk through the page and left a mark on the next.

'Why?'

Leo simply closed his eyes. The crevices deepened. Every part of his body seemed tense, seemed almost ready to shatter. There was no answer for this one. I saw his lips move, attempting to form words, to say something that would lessen the pain, that would somehow, someway, explain it all. Explain all that was unexplainable. Abandonment. Loneliness. Death. But where was the life? Where was Leo's life?

I wished that I could have found some words, found anything at all, but what was the point? So fixed was Leo's denial, that even though the pain had resurfaced for a moment, he would soon suppress it again. Push it deep down into himself, and patch up the hole with mere definitions, mere generalities, that knew nothing of the truth of the world.

Why?

This was the very question that had ignited Leo's obsession with the dictionary. With the dictionary, came Leo's discovery that he could escape the horrors of the world, escape his wife's abandonment, escape the inevitable tragedies in life. But it also meant resigning himself to a life of ink and paper, in which he would never know the true answer to that question - "why?" - in which, not only would the tragedy be lost, but the happiness as well. Everything in life, the good and the bad, is all tangled up like a ball of string. It is impossible to make sense of, impossible to untangle, but that's the greatness of it, isn't it?

When Leo had fallen asleep. I reached over and pulled the old copy of *The Oxford Paperback Dictionary* out of the drawer in the bedside table where I knew it would be, and thumbed through it absentmindedly. My eyes alighted on the word "loneliness", beside which, Leo had written his own name, "Leopold Bernstein" in bold capital letters.

4. to cease gradually.

Contributors

Meleina Backhaus
Meleina Backhaus was born in Belle Fourche South Dakota at the start of the 80's. She barely remembers it but feels she has been scarred by a pink scrunchie. She writes purely from thinking about things, and her inspiration comes solely from whatever happens to be in her head at the time. She enjoys Earl Grey tea to a ridiculous degree, and is a master at making Hot Chocolate. She is extremely excited to be included in this Anthology.

Shannon Bates
Shannon Bates is a San Diego musician and writer with over twenty years of experience in each area. She earned a Bachelor of Music (composition) from Pacific Lutheran University in Tacoma, Washington, and has been a very active saxophone player and fiction writer in the San Diego community for twelve years. She has played sax and flute in groups of vastly varying styles, including an afrobeat/funk band called Society, which was nominated for Best New Artist at the 2007 San Diego Music Awards. She has been a featured writer at several poetry and fiction readings throughout Southern California. Much of her poetry and a handful of her short stories have been published in the *Acorn Review* and in *Saxifrage*, among other small journals and newsletters. She is currently pitching her completed young adult novel called *The Ugly House*, and she is working on at least three new book-length projects.

Digby Beaumont
Digby Beaumont lives by the seaside, in Brighton on the south coast of England. He taught sociology and English in his twenties before working as a freelance nonfiction author for many years, with numerous

publications. Now he writes mainly short fiction. His work has been published widely in literary magazines and journals: *Leafing Through, Barfing Frog Press, The Raging Face, Zygote in My Coffee*, Laura Hird's *Showcase, Whim's Place* and *The Scruffy Dog Review*, among others. His stories have also been chosen to appear in print anthologies: 'A Real Woman' in *Small Voices, Big Confessions* (Edit Red) and 'All Right As We Are' in *On a Whim* (Whim's Place). 'Dreaming of Kathy Burke' won the Spoiled Ink Writer's Choice Award for July 2006.

Chris Bell

Chris bell was born in Wales. Shrugging off this early setback, he moved from Holyhead to Hamburg, via London, in a futile search for any of the trappings of rock superstardom, before arriving in New Zealand where, having gone as far as he could, he now works as a writer. His short stories have appeared in *The Third Alternative*; *Grotesque*; *The Heidelberg Review*; *Transversions*; *Zahir*; *Postscripts*; *Not One of Us*; and *Takahe*, as well as on the internet, which you can get on your computer, apparently. The Cruel Countess was anthologised in *The Year's Best Fantasy & Horror* (10th Annual Edition), published by St Martin's Griffin Books, in which his collection The Bumper Book of Lies received an Honourable Mention. He was editor of a technology management magazine for five-and-a-half years, but failed to recognise the widespread adoption of the mobile phone and is now unfashionably out of range. His first novel, *Liquidambar* won the UKAuthors/PADB 'Great Read' Novel Writing competition. He is currently working on a second novel, *Saccade*.

Dan Coxon

Dan Coxon is a freelance journalist and writer, and the author of the Wee Book Of Scotland. He contributes regularly to *Is This Music?* and *Rock'n'Reel* magazines, although his work has appeared in a variety of publications, from the *Scottish Cricketer* to the *3:AM* website. He has recently moved to Tacoma, Washington.

William de Rham
Born and raised in New York City, William de Rham is a graduate of Georgetown University and the University of California, Hastings College of the Law. His work has appeared or is forthcoming in *RiverSedge, Broken Bridge Review, Puckerbrush Review, Ascent Aspirations, Fiction on the Web, Pulse, New Works Review*, and an urban anthology soon to be published by EditRED. He lives in Maine where he is at work on two novels and more stories.

Lauren Farnsworth
Lauren Farnsworth was born in Essex, England in 1985. She attained her degree in Fine Art at Central Saint Martins College in London, and studied Creative Writing with Joanna Pocock. Previously, she has been published in *Rock Sound, Delivered,* and in several of her local news publications. She is currently living with her partner in Kent and working on her first novel. In her spare time she enjoys playing scrabble and drinking copies amounts of tea.

Tom Gant
Tom Gant was born in Yorkshire, England. He currently resides by the Humber Estuary, where he studies for an MA in English and Creative Writing, and passes his spare time writing poetry and experimenting with photography. His short fiction and poetry have appeared in *Small Voices, Big Confessions*: EditRED's 2006 short story anthology, *Citizen 32 magazine*, and innumerable ezines.

Like all writers, Tom is currently working on a novel and hopes to have it rejected across the UK publishing board sometime before Easter 2008.

Paolo Gardinali
Paolo Gardinali does not remember a time of his life when he did not enjoy writing, drawing or simply telling stories. He is currently working on an anthology of dystopian California stories, a novel for young (but smart) adults and a biography of his dog.

Lawrence M. John

Lawrence M. John was raised, shaped and moulded on the Medway, England. Once Upon a Time the Medway Literati is his first story to be published.

Jreamwriter

Having been compared the world renowned Jamaica Kincaid, Jreamwriter has received acclamations internationally for her writings.

Jreamwriter attended Brookdale College in Monmouth County, New Jersey and studied journalism under adjunct, Arthur Z. Kamin, independent journalist for the Asbury Park Press, and creative writing, under Professor Jeffery Ford, famous author of 'The Girl In The Glass' and 'The Portrait of Mrs. Charbuque'.

Born and raised in New York City, Jreamwriter is an (ex) web developer/computer graphics designer and currently resides in Atlanta, Georgia, where she has completed her debut novel titled, 'The Rainbow Through The Eyes Of A Closet Homosexual's Wife' which is released January 2008 and available for purchase at book retailers worldwide and online at BarnesandNobles.com and Amazon.com.

Bernadette Klubb

Bernadette Klubb was lucky enough to be born and reared in the very heart of Fairyland, otherwise known as The Kingdom of Mourne on the eastern coast of Northern Ireland, and many of her characters are drawn from the larger-than-life community that breathed a love of literature into her at a very early age.

Her two most valued literary lessons came from a mother who counselled boiling one's head and shaking the bones out of it as a cure for literary block and a father whose credo was "Never spoil the telling of a good yarn by worrying about things like the truth." When she manages to follow both these ground rules, the result can sometimes be entertaining.

Bernadette is currently scouring the Midi-Pyrénées in search of a new home away from the bustle of South East England where she lived for the previous 30 years. A place, where hopefully the slower pace of life will be more reminiscent of her early youth and allow her more time to write, garden and grow old gracefully.

Her story in last year's EditRED anthology, *Small Voices, Big Confessions*, was chosen from her fairy collection.

Matthew Louis
Matthew Louis edits, illustrates, publishes and contributes to the underground pulp magazine *Out of the Gutter*. He is currently putting the finishing touches on a novel.

James Meredith
James Meredith, from Belfast, Northern Ireland, is a past winner & runner-up of the Brian Moore Short Story Award. His work has appeared in various anthologies & literary journals in Ireland, the UK & the USA, including *Small Voices, Big Confessions* from EditRED Press.

Anne Leigh Parrish
Anne Leigh Parrish's short stories have appeared or are forthcoming in *The Virginia Quarterly Review, New Century Voices, Clackamas Literary Review* (winning the Willamette Award in Fiction), *Carve Magazine, Fiction Warehouse, River Walk Journal, Amarillo Bay, Eclectica Magazine, Lunch Hour Stories*, and elsewhere. She was named a Finalist in *Glimmer Train*'s Summer 2007 Fiction Open, *Salt Flat*'s Annual 2007 Emerging Writer Fiction Contest, both the 2006 and 2005 Arts & Letters Prize, *Meridian*'s 2004 Editors' Prize, and *Painted Bride Quarterly*'s 2003 Fiction Contest. She lives in Seattle, Washington and has taught creative writing at both the University of Washington Women's Center, and the Richard Hugo.

Jessica Phippen

Jessica Phippen is a student living in London. The Dictionary of Loneliness is her first published piece. She also has a story entitled New York City Blackout in Columbia University's monthly online magazine *The Urban Reinventors*. She is preparing to attend university, where she wants to study English and Visual Arts. She hopes to one day become a teacher and an author. Her favourite writers include Jonathan Safran Foer, E.M. Forster, Zadie Smith and William Shakespeare. She hopes to one day be a poet as well, but she's still struggling with that particular goal. She has three cats, a dog, loves Gustave Caillebotte's "Les Raboteurs de Parquet" and The Shins.

Samantha Priestly

Samantha Priestley was born in Sheffield, England, where she still lives today. She is 36 and married with two children. Her short stories have appeared in the magazines *Take a Break Fiction Feast* in the UK, *Conceit* in the US and *Saley Publications* in Canada, as well as *Espresso Fiction* online. She was runner up in the Mike Hayward competition and *The Pages* competition, highly commended in The Shrewsbury Literary prize and short-listed for the Sid Chaplin award. Her first novel, Despite Losing it on Finkle Street, was chosen as the launch title for the new imprint, Pioneer Readers, at Fygleaves publishing, and is on sale now.

T. Rigney

T. Rigney unleashed his first novel, 2004's coming of age horror opus Found, to the deafening sound of zealous crickets chirping in the distance. "Relative obscurity," he often remarks, "is actually quite relaxing, if not a tad confining." When he isn't planning the big comeback of a career that never was, he spends his time waxing intellectual about cult cinema at *TheFilmFiend.com*. He's married, an unsightly shade of pale, and not quite ready for thirty.

Teri Davis Rouvelas

Born in South Dakota and a member of the Turtle Mountain Band of Ojibwe, Teri Davis Rouvelas was raised in Rhode Island where she is implanted for life. She is the mother of two grown children, Krystan and Tom. Teri is currently in the process of finishing her Bachelors Degree and is the oldest thing in the classroom including the dust. However, she loves every minute of it because her age makes her fellow students think she's full of wisdom. She spends her days writing and slowly becoming one of those weird cat ladies with the funny fruit hats.

Alice Shin

Alice Shin is a twenty-something Californian who enjoys long walks on sandy beaches, inexpensive dining, and free drinks. Dislikes: sand, cheap food, and random strangers purchasing her beverages for no apparent reason. She is currently looking for a reader who has a tolerance for weirdness and gender and racial subtext. For those on the literary prowl for weirdness and gender and racial subtext, Shin's work can be found on EditRED.com and has been previously published in *34th Parallel* and EditRED.com's *City Smells* Anthology. Personal checks and money orders of appreciation of Shin's literary genius are always welcome and will be gladly received by EditRED.com's editors, who will gladly wire them to Shin's bank account. Gladly.

Stacy Taylor

Stacy Taylor lives in the wilds of Alaska, writing, gardening, and practicing photography. Her writing has appeared in many web and print publications and her photography has appeared on the covers of three books. She is currently working on two novels, both of which dip into the murky waters of speculative fiction.

http://www.stacytaylor.net

Nisha Woolfstein
Before graduating from Cambridge University this year, Nisha Woolfstein lived and worked Asia, Australia the United States, Mexico and Spain. She has published travel articles and is currently writing her first novel.

Sarah Young
Sarah Young is currently a Senior Writing for Film and Television major at the University of the Arts in Philadelphia, PA. Having loved writing since the first grade, her ultimate dream is to be a writer on a television show for a major network, to win an Emmy, and to write an award-winning screenplay. She would also like to write a novel, but that's always easier said than done. So for now, she is sticking to short stories. This is her first publication.

www.ingramcontent.com/pod-product-compliance
Lightning Source LLC
Chambersburg PA
CBHW030332030726
47499CB00003B/741